DEAD
LIEUTENANT
IN TAMPA

RICHARD SCHMIDT

authorHOUSE®

AuthorHouse™
1663 Liberty Drive
Bloomington, IN 47403
www.authorhouse.com
Phone: 1-800-839-8640

Published by AuthorHouse   10/13/2014

ISBN: 978-1-4969-4559-4 (sc)
ISBN: 978-1-4969-4558-7 (e)

Library of Congress Control Number: 2014918078

CONTENTS

Afghanistan 2001

Zulu 3 to Zulu leader I've been hit. Zulu leader to Zulu 3 can you continue to fly?" Negative, lost control have to pop out."

"Roger that we have you spotted."

The pilot pulled hard on his ejection lever and was catapulted over Afghanistan watching his F-15 spiral down on fire. His parachute was open and he floated down hitting the rocky ground with a thud. He unhooked his harness and was free from the parachute. Feeling a rush of fear he pushed himself to remember his training the U.S. Air Force had drilled into his every being. Grabbing his 9mm from his holster he ran for a cluster of rocks for cover and hit his beacon praying to God that he would survive this catastrophe. The Taliban was close, he was sure of that. He gathered the chute, pulled off his helmet and piled sand over them trying to prevent detection from around him. The pilot knew this would be the end if he was captured. Then out of the dust appeared a miracle. There stood a muscular friendly wearing his BDU's and maroon beret with his M-4 slung out to do battle with a portable radio in his right hand.

Combat Controller Staff Sergeant Daniel Burns had been watching the pilot descend and was already calling for a Pararecsue helicopter to extract them both. Burns had been in the area setting up the air strike the young pilot had been a part of. "You got most of them Lieutenant with your first run" Burns grinned as he made the statement. "There's a few hostiles still in the area but there aware if they come out to soon the rest of your air squad up there is waiting to swope down on them". The pilot shook his head in agreement with this. He knew the choppers better get there quick as the rest of the F-15s limited fuel to keep cover for him. Within a few minutes a rescue helicopter hovered and came down to extract the pilot and Sergeant. Burns pulled the pilot up and pushed him toward the open door of the chopper. Once on board the gunner fired a burst to ensure no hostiles made an attempt to charge at them. The rotors lifted the big machine up and the crew medic checked for any injuries to the fallen pilot and they made across the sky to safety.

CHAPTER - 1

The Netherlands 2014

The meeting took place outside of Amsterdam in a private mansion. The meeting was a mandatory two day and night affair. The men and women who attended were the leaders of the secret group "Stahl." They were an assorted cast. Many were politicians, lawyers, bankers, leaders of industry, oil men, former military Generals and of even a single religous scholar. They were from different countries, but their allegiance was to the group. Every man and women in attendance controlled vast amounts of wealth. They had advanced educations, and influence. The group had one goal, to control the world, its riches, and its populations. They had no desire to better mankind, but to enslave them, control them and be the master. They attempted to control world events behind the scenes. Causing mayhem, financial desperation, political upheaval, wars, and revolutions was the trade mark they specialized.

The leaders of the secret society were bankers Joachim Lebovitch, his brother Herman and socialite sister Sarah. They were cruel people as were the others. They believed in no god for they considered themselves gods. The brothers and sister were known in the group for their sadistic sexual appetites, leaving casualties jet setting around the world. The group had people in powerful positions who they controlled. They influenced the activities of world governments, for their long range plan to control the world on their terms. They used organized crime and dictators to do the dirty work, keeping their hands clean. Their activities were always behind the scenes. The members voted by committee on resolutions and strategic plans.

Sarah Lebovitch, a shrewd woman, considered herself the princess of the world. She was upset at the course of the last few years and felt the group had been set back in its goals. The last few years, the resurgence of nationalist pride in the Middle East, Asia, and Africa had created chaos with the plans the group had for the world. Sarah had come up with a devious plan to accelerate the groups path for control and domination of the world. After a cocktail party and a five course meal the group gathered in the lecture room of the mansion and Sarah spoke to them from a podium

She was a beautiful looking women and mesmerized the group as she spoke to them

---

"My esteemed collages, we are the people of steel, we are the saviors of the world, we are the gods, people so desperately worship. We have created the world, we know best how things should be. The people of the world are weak and stupid. Without our guidance the world would be lost. Recently our plans have had a set back with the events in the Middle East, Africa, and Asia. The people have become unruly and have attempted to establish religious jihads and some others, free market democracy. Due to the interference of people we couldn't control we have seen a pattern in the east we can no longer tolerate. Our use of terrorism and conventional warfare has stalled and created road blocks. Therefore I have a plan to right our course and speed up events."

The group looked on with interest as Sarah was captivating in looks and her delivery was always spell binding.

"A criminal organization under the direction of one Demetri Stanasoksky has its tentacles in Europe, Canada and America. There foray is drug smuggling and other assorted criminal ventures. The smuggling business is the important aspect of the plan I have developed. We will pay Mr. Stanasolsky to smuggle three nuclear suitcase into the capitals of Iran, Pakistan and Sudan. The suitcases will be stolen from a military installation in Maryland and shipped to Tampa by our people in the Pentagon. The theft will be covered up by substituting phony suitcases in their place. Once the bombs are smuggled out of the country and detonated by Stanasolsky' people, we will use our influences in these countries to place our people in leadership positions, use martial law and inject our goals into daily government. The world will blame terrorism and with the destruction created, the common man will want a return to a normal life at any cost and accept the new governments controlled by us. No connection or trace of our operations will exist. The criminal Stanasolsky, his smuggling organization, and a well know terrorist organization will be identified as the culprit after a proper period of time. They will be blamed and destroyed while we sit back and watch. My brother Herman will make contact with Mr. Stanasolsky and persuade him with an intoxicating amount of money, he will not be able to turn down. We will use our people in the American C.I.A. and the military to keep an eye on things and ensure they go as planned."

The group applauded Sarah and agreed the plan was a master piece.

Tampa Florida 2014 Davis Island an exclusive gated Community.

Demetri Stanasolsky drank his glass of vodka with vigor. He looked out to the beautiful Gulf of Mexico from his ten million dollar American Home. Demetri was the king of his castle he was the King of the Russians, Serbs, and Albanians that worked for him in Tampa. He owned two big topless clubs and ran protection rackets some in Miami and some in Tampa. He wanted more and he would get it. Demetri knew the more powerful he was the longer he would stay on top and he intended to always remain on top. The Russian vodka and its smooth taste was like that of a beautiful women's lips. Vodka was what kept Stanasolsky alive in the Russian winters when the winds blew over the steppe and through the small farm house on the collective. Stanasolsky worked the fields for the state and then when he was seventeen he was drafted into the Red Army and after his training school was a soldier of occupation in Warsaw Poland. Demetri was

5

quick to make money by helping other Russian soldiers extort and steal from the Polish people. After the Soviet Empire collapsed from the corruption and cruel rule over the Russian people Demetri returned home to Moscow from the newly freed Poland. Demetri tried to make a life in the new Russia, but it was corrupt and dangerous. The country was hardened by the years of communism. The former KGB and Red Army commanders became the new Russian Mafia. Demetri was a solider in the Mafia working the streets of Moscow as a debt collector and a drug supplier. Heroin from the fields of Afghanistan with the ability of Demetri to buy, sell, and command an empire of drugs supplying Europe made him rich beyond his dreams. Then the new President of Russia using the power of the secret police and the paramilitary police put Demetri on trial and sent him to a Russian Prison for several years. Demetri survived and when he paid enough euros to the corrupt government he was allowed to leave the prison. He applied to the Americans for help telling them he was a political prisoner and would be jailed or even killed for his religious beliefs and his protest against the Russian President. He was permitted to immigrate to the America after stops in west Europe and Israel. The final prize was making it to America. The Americans were stupid and would believe anyone that said the right things. They were soft and wanted to believe in everyone. Demetri was a master manipulator. He arrived in America and then tapped into the Eastern European Community and began his criminal life in America, using the money he had hidden in the many countries of Europe. Before long Demetri was thriving. He couldn't believe the Americans; their Criminal Justice system was wonderful. Justice for the criminal. Enough money to the dirty lawyers and cops, kept the problems to a minimum. The American criminals were weak and they always snitched on each other to stop a longer prison sentence. These so called American gangsters could never survive a Russian Gulag. There were several criminal families in Tampa that Demetri needed to destroy and put his style of fear in them. His empire would be the only one, he would rule the city no one else was going to be a threat to him. Demetri used his fruitful diamond mine in Afghanistan under the noise of the Americans to bank roll the Afghanistan heroin he smuggled into these great United States. The heroin was the best and he had the city addicts lining up for the product. Since the Americans had invaded Afghanistan the Taliban and the other Afghan tribes increased their production and sale of the drug to fiancé the fight against the Worlds armies in their country. Demetri's organization paid the Taliban in cash for the heroin he smuggled to the United States and Canada. Demetri's power was growing and he was getting more powerful as the days past. Demetri enjoyed only the finest in life. He had installed himself in a luxury waterfront home in

/HANDLE

Tampa on Davis Island, where the elite lived. Demetri was living the life he had carved out for himself by being the stronger and wiser criminal in a world run by the weak.

Demetri enjoyed the fine things in life and today was no different. He entered his favorite restaurant, a Tampa Steak house that served only the finest cuts of beef. He drank the best Russian vodka the restaurant carried. Demetri was far away from the Russian gulag he had survived. Life was wonderful for him, but he knew he must always keep in mind the lessons he learned from the cruel Soviet system.

A man dressed impeccably appeared at the table. He extended his hand as a friendly gesture and identified himself as Mr. Jones, but Demetri knew right away it not his real name. He sat down at the table and Demetri waved his body guard away. Mr. Jones had an air confidence and a calm quiet voice with a hint of an accent Demetri couldn't make out.

He ordered brandy and began to talk to Demetri "Mr. Stanasolsky I am so sorry to interrupt you while you are dining, but I have a very important business deal to discuss with you. Demetri was impressed with the man's style and the fact that only a few people knew Demetri was in Tampa. So he listened to the mysterious man as he ate his expensive steak dinner and sipped his vodka.

The man sat back and began "I represent a very powerful group of people who have interest in business, government and politics. The people I represent will remain unnamed, but rest assured they have authorized me to make a very profitable deal with you. Mr. Stanasolsky we are well aware of you, your background, and your smuggling criminal enterprise. We know you have criminal operations in Europe and have recently come to the United States and Canada. You control the Miami area and have come to Tampa recently to expand. The police have been only a minor problem to you, and of course the people I represent have no fear of the police. We also are aware of the contacts and employees you have working all over the world. Your organization is very impressive. Therefore we want to do business with you. We will pay you handsomely for your services. If you decide not to work for us, we will understand. We would then be forced to use someone else in your line of work. We do want you for the job. Your lack of cooperation could make you an enemy of my employers, which could be a problem for you in the future."

Demetri put his fork down and sipped his vodka. The last words were a threat. He looked at the confident stare of

Mr. Jones and for the first time in a long time felt fear. Demetri remained calm but he could feel his anxiety rising. He asked "Why me, why do you come to me for my services, why not others ?"

"Frankly Mr. Stanasolsky you're a dependable man who we feel we can trust. So many of the men and women in your line of work are undependable and cannot be trusted. We also know your organization has connections in the middle east where we want you to act for us. Would you care for me to continue?"

Demetri nodded his head and said "Go on."

You realize my associates want no link to you or your activities. You will be tasked to use your organization to smuggle three nuclear suitcases out of the United States and into Tehran Iran, Karachi Pakistan, and Khartoum Sudan. Then you will have your people detonate them when you're directed by me.

Demetri looked horrified at the man and said "Why would I do this, money would do me no good if the world destroys itself, I would be out of business hiding in a bomb shelter. No this is not what Demetri does, Demetri will not live in a bomb shelter.

"On the contrary Mr. Stanasolsky this will not only make you rich with the money my clients pay you, but it will increase your business. Like I explained to you, the people I represent have plans to put their own people into power in these countries, people who will cooperate with my clients and of course you and your associates. With the change in these countries completed, business can then be done as usual. The climate of these nations is very dark, they each have a strategic location in regards to doing business with China and the rest of the world. They are causing trouble with their damn jihad and there refusal to accept and adapt to the western way. Once the plan is completed these countries will have new leadership who can be counted on to liberate the people and open them up to doing business with a civilized society. You will be allowed to carry on your activities and my associates will ensure your business ventures, accelerate. We are aware people will always want what you sell and we would like to see you prosper for your services. My clients encourage your type of business to help control society from becoming to righteous. We are prepared to pay you a five hundred million dollars. The money will be transferred to a Swiss bank account established by you. Of course if you think of trying to double cross us you will not live long and your organization will be destroyed."

Demetri knew this man was telling him the truth. He had seen the cold stare of the communist in his country of Russia. They controlled everything, even to this day in the name of free market. Demetri was a business man, the people of world loved narcotics and vice and that's what Demetri supplied. Now here was a chance to earn a billion dollars smuggling nuclear suit case bombs into these throw back countries. The thought of the money was intoxicating. The instant wealth would propel Demetri to the top of the criminal world. These people came to Demetri, they knew he was the best. It would be good to be in business with them. He had survived the gulag by being crafty, he would survive these people and maybe end up controlling them. Why not take their money and use it to his advantage.

Demetri finished the wine, looked at Mr. Jones and said, "you have a deal with Demetri".

Mr. Jones smiled and stood up. He extended his hand to Demetri and said "Wonderful I will contact the group I represent and you will receive your payment in installments, half now and half when you complete the transaction. I will be in touch with you to check on your plans for execution of our agreement and coordinate the particulars. Goodnight for now, Demetri."

He drank the cold vodka and after tedious thought came up with a plan to carry out the the smuggling and detonation of the nuclear suit cases to the destinations directed by Mr. Jones. Demetri would use former, Russian military commandos, now trusted mafia members, to enter the United States without detection and have them deliver the suitcases to the locations. Demetri then had a brilliant idea. He would slay another dragon. While the men were in America undetected, he would have these men destroy his criminal competitors in Tampa and rule the streets. Demetri was overcome with ecstasy at the good fortune he was having. The city of Tampa would yield to his rule and soon he would control the underworld.

Demetri awoke to a new day, he left his bed and walked out on to the expensive tiled patio and jumped into the swimming pool. The was cool and he did his best thinking while floating in the pool. He had to take care of a problem which had raised its ugly head so there would be no unnecessary problems geeting in the way of his work for Mr. Jones and his organization. A greedy American Military Officer, a bitch who worked with his organization had become greedy and demanded more money for her work. She was useful with her access to classified and secret information. She was key to providing information about American military patrols interfering with heroine smuggling routes used by his organization in Afghanistan. Her information helped his drug operation flourish overseas. She had been transferred back to America, to MacDill Air Force Base in Tampa, and continued to use her position to help the organization smuggle dope into the cities of Tampa and Miami. Then she demanded a grotesque amount of money to continue her work, and even threatened Demetri's operations. No one did that and lived, no matter if they were important or not. The information she supplied had been invaluable, but somebody else in her position would be found and bribed. She was to become an example to others who thought about making demands.

Demetri pressed the button on his cell phone to call Boris Kolovos a former KGB agent who ran the operations of the organization and answered only to Demetri

Boris answered the phone and Demetri explained to him the lucrative and detailed plan to carry out the contract from Mr. Jones. When he was done with the particulars he added the pesky problem of the Air force Lieutenant.

"One more thing Boris ... Kill the American Lieutenant working for us. She was paid generously for her services. She now demands more money. She challenges me, Demetri..... she will cause me problems, if she does not get her way. The bitch. She is not to be trusted. No one tells Demetri he must pay more."

Boris waited until Demetri had finished and replied "She will be dead before you awake in the morning my friend."

Tampa Florida 2012 Police Headquarters

Detective Lieutenant Dan Burns sat at his desk and read the daily reports from the Narcotics, Vice, C.I.D., Burglary, Homicide and Robbery divisions. Tampa Florida was a busy place for crime and criminals. Everybody was trying to get over anyway they could. It didn't matter who. Burns was in charge of the Special Investigation Unit. When he separated from active duty from the Air force he was recruited by the C.I.A. spending several years doing clandestine work in countries he had a hard time pronouncing. His training as an air force combat controller which included jungle school, survival school, cold weather training, tours in Iraq and Afghanistan, made the training and work at the C.I.A. an easy transition. After the politics of the government started to wear on him, he decided to take a job as a Police Officer. He needed the action of a fast pace in his life and Tampa P.D. was more than happy to hire him with his education and profound experience, after a short compliance course, along with his military and federal schooling he was a sworn member of Tampa's finest. Dan liked what he was doing he felt that he made a difference to the regular Joe on the street. Justice was something Dan really believed in not so much the law but justice for people that had been wronged by force's they couldn't fight but the police could. Seeing the little person bullied really got to Dan and being a cop was his way of helping those who were in need. The courts were of course run by the lawyers and most of them only believed in how much money they could make, the criminals, cops and the victims were just pawns in the system, possible revenue. Watching the lawyers in court was frustrating, cutting deals with criminals and letting them take the easy way out, but that was reality and Dan knew you had to accept it and continue to find ways of making the streets safe within the context of the law. He believed in justice not the law.

He excelled and was promoted over a period of a few years and then the Chief of Police seeing his talents, put him in charge of the S.I.U. The unit consisted of six veteran officers, Sergeant Michael Hanson and Corporal Jack Bradley, who were smart, trust worthy, worked as a team along with Officers Denise Ramstein, Bill Barton, Ron Becker, and Johnny Creasy. The unit worked passionately and closed many cases. The unit roamed the city and did street surveillance in high crime areas watching and responding. They gathered and analyzed information from wire taps, informants, stakeouts, interviews, they kept an eye on organized crime in the city including drug dealers, gypsies, biker gangs and the new Russian mob that had arrived in Tampa and were spreading their tentacles. The information was then passed on to the Police Bureau Chiefs and the State Attorney who directed cases to be made if they felt they had enough to prosecute. When there was a case the Tampa Police Chief wanted to be dealt with outside regular channels, S.I.U was assigned the task.

The members of the squad respected and liked Burns, he was fair and just commander. He also demanded each member of his unit play by the rules, stay focused on the law and what they were doing. The main rule was to be careful, objective, treat people as fair as possible, and never take anything personal. Dan was always available at any time for any member of the unit if they needed him for any reason and they knew it. Dan would back them with the brass and understood they had a very tough job. The work was long hours and did wear one down at times. Each officer was encouraged to take vacation so as not to get mental burn out. Dan believed in time off when needed and he was going to practice that benefit starting the next day, two weeks of vacation at his Clearwater Beach condominium. Lisa Jones Assistant State Prosecutor his love interest had scheduled time off from her office to help Dan live it up on the beach and in his bed. He smiled and could already feel the sand between his toes and the cool water of the beach. Time with Lisa was so relaxing.

The water was cool and very calm. Dan and Lisa bobbed in the water, enjoying the warm rays of the sun on their already tan bodies. Lisa was long and curvy; she filled her white bathing suit with her beautiful attributes. Dan muscles bulged naturally, he was hard and fit from years of weights training and jogging.

Lisa wrapped her arms around Dan's neck and asked "Do you think we should quit are jobs and stay here on this beach forever?"

Dan looked at her smiled and said, "Counselor you could never stay away from the grim and dark halls of justice. Your one of the good guys, who knows that the system needs and depends on the few in it, who have common sense and care about the people you serve. Lisa you are married to the job because your passionate about what justice is. Your not the typical greedy lawyer who spends a year as a prosecutor and then jumps into private practice to make a millon dollars by getting off guilty as hell people. You enjoy helping the victims which the courts forget about and seeing the criminal has the day they deserve. You'll always be a prosecutor with compassion and a steel will. Hey that's why I love you so much."

Lisa looked hard into Dan's eyes and kissed him long and with meaning. She pulled back after the kiss and said, "You know your just as passionate about your work. That's what so attractive about you stud. Oh and don't ever forget your mine, the man I love and desire. Come on lets go back to the condo, where I can show you my passion for you."

CHAPTER - 2

The street light were they parked was out. Dan and Johnny Creasy watched with binoculars. A black man hung on the corner with his eye out for the next expensive car to direct into the "retail area". The area was government housing known as the Gardens. It was home to low no income folks with no future. The only thing that the area offered was vice. Prostitutes roamed the streets and the independent drug pushers waited for the kid from the burbs to drive in and get there take out. The menu was heroin, meth, crack cocaine, oxy, pot, and the new drug known as "molly". Lately the worst had come to the Gardens and all over Tampa, Afghan heroin was the new enemy the Russian gangsters brought to Tampa making them rich. The war in Afghanistan had not stopped the drug from being smuggled to America. The new appetite of the drug users in Tampa and other cities made heroin the most sought after drug. The Gardens were always busy.

Several cars pulled up to the corner of the Gardens and a tall black man would look at them and wave them into the housing project. Once in the square of apartments the trade of money for drugs or stolen property for drugs would be exchanged. Kids would come into the gardens with their mother's microwaves for a handful of crack or a vile of cocaine. The junkies appetite for heroin was fast becoming a problem in the city. The officials and the Police Department were grasping to get a handle on the epidemic. Officer Johnny Creasy sat with a digital recorder and filmed it all. "Look at these jackasses, they would sell their soul for that shit" said Creasy. Creasy was a former Army Ranger from Louisiana. He came to Tampa on a vacation and joined the police department after realizing her never wanted to leave Tampa. He was coy, intelligent and a hard charger. Johnny was Latin from his mother and Cajun from his father. He had excelled in patrol and was a great fit for Dan's squad. Nobody fooled Johnny Creasy.

"Just find me the stash and sale house Johnny, and S.W.A.T. will raid it. Then hope the next one doesn't open to fast", replied Dan. A blue S.U.V. pulled up and Creasy stopped the filming.

"Lieutenant the women buying dope is the wife of a guy who works patrol. I know her," Creasy had concern in his voice.

Dan looked at the women handing the money out of her window and said to Creasy, "Let's finish up the movie work and when we get back to the office call your friend in patrol and tell him his wife needs to get some help."

Creasy smiled and said "10-4".

After several days of surveillance and many buys of dope by narcotics detectives making cases by doing hand to hand buys, Creasy noticed a reinforced steel door on an apartment on the first floor of the units in a corner building on the grounds of the Gardens. The door never opened until it was dark and then the usual dealers made a short visit inside. Creasy contacted Corporal Jack Bradley by cell phone telling him with exuberance "Bingo we found the prize, I'm certain we found the stash and sale house Jack. We have a corner apartment that is walled up tighter than Fort Knox.

"I'll call Sergeant Hanson and tell him what you observed, Johnny you sure this is the real thing? Bradley replied.

Johnny firmly said "We gotta do these dealers brother, and besides its time to let them know who runs the show and close their shop."

Bradley rolled his eyes, but tried to remember when he was a young cop full of optimism about changing the city for the better, Bradley restrained himself from lecturing and said, "yeah Johnny will let em know but as soon as their out of business there will be another one hundred to take up where they left off. So relax and don't get yourself killed over a bunch of scum drug dealers, the life insurance the city pays is lousy."

The S.W.A.T team rolled into the gardens at about 5:00 a.m,the time when even the dealers and addicts found time to get some rest from their desperate seedy life. The team of heavily armored special tactics police hit the door with the thump of the long metal ramming pole attached to the front of their armored vehicle. The two teams rushed through the battered door that lay flat, tossed a flash bang inside the drug den and quickly took control of the occupants in the apartment. The individuals inside the apartment were stunned and lay on the floor dazed by the noise, smoke. They responsed to the commands of the heavily armed police to put their hands behind their backs and shut up. When it was all secured three thugs were cuffed and stuffed and an array of hand guns, a shotgun and two fully automatic AK47'S were confiscated from the apartment. Sergeant Michael Hanson and Jack Bradley of S.I.U stood with a Sergeant from Narcotics and were amazed at what they were surrounded by. The room contained at least ten million dollars worth of Afghan heroine. The men that were arrested in the apartment appeared to be two Serbians who refused to give their names. The third man was known to police, Biker Gus "Smiley" Baker a member of the Satan's Wolves Motorcycle Club. The Biker, Baker was found to have had in his right boot a .45 automatic pistol which was confiscated when he was patted down and taken into evidence. None of them would make any statement and denied knowing anything. They were booked and jailed.

A call went to the home of Boris, the caller was brief but clear," they hit a stash and sale house and found a score. Our product is lost but we have four other houses working steady."

Boris knew he must call Demetri, as unpleasant as it would be to tell the man the American police had taken his property.

Chapter - 3

Dawn Ross and Robert Sherman drove out of the main gate of MacDill A.F.B. They were on their way to meet Boris at a club in Ybor City. The meeting had been arranged by Boris to talk to Dawn about her demand for more money. Robert also worked for Demetri and had been recruited by Dawn in Afghanistan while stationed there. They both had the ambition to get rich. It was an ends to the mean in their minds, and they had no problem working for criminals.

Robert the F-15 pilot, would alert Dawn on classified Air operations targeting Taliban smuggling routes. She would contact Savvy and he would pass the information on to Demetri's heroin smugglers dealing with the Taliban. Dawn grew up in a middle income family in Los Angles California. Her parents had adopted her, and given her a good life. She appreciated them, but never felt close to them. She had a photographic memory and school was easy for her. Her goal was to see the world and be rich. She excelled through college and decided she would become an AirForce Officer, gain status and get paid to travel to faraway lands. She enlisted and entered Officers Candidate School. Her opportunity was her fate. Fresh out of her Officers training school, a commissioned Second Lieutenant, and top of her class in military intelligence school. Dawn was extremely ambitious, but she wanted to be independent and wealthy. She knew the AirForce was the means to an end. Training was over and she received orders to Afghanistan, an assignment to a secure listening post, providing drones with targets to destroy the enemy and gather intelligence to pass on to special forces, coalition, and Afghan army units on daily patrol. Her journey stated by departing on a commericial flight from Kennedy Airport and landing in Amsterdam's Schiphol Airport to change flights. Due to bad weather she was delayed for two days. There in the one of the many airport bars she met Savvy, a large good looking, well dressed, Russian traveler. After several drinks, some laughs, and to much anxiety thinking about a year to spend in Afghanistan, she spent the night with him in the airport hotel. After having sex, they lay in bed relaxed, sipping whiskey from a bottle of bush mills from the duty free airport shop, she told him of her desire to be rich and travel. She told him of her military training and where she was going to be stationed. She had mixed feelings about the war against terrorism, questioning the death of so many people while the industrialists and the bankers became rich. The handsome Russian told her of his business, he was an importer exporter for an organization. They supplied people with what they wanted to be happy, selling pleasure, and making a fortune. Savvy and Dawn agreed to stay in touch. Savvy spoke to his superiors about the girl. They agreed she could be used to their advantage with her position in military intelligence. Dawn was contacted by Savvy via her e-mail and being disillusioned about the war, and fed up with the Spartan life style she was living in Afghanistan, she accepted Savvy's offer to sell him information he needed about heroin fields that were abundant and the best physical access to them, avoiding military patrols. Dawn and Robert both finished their tour in Afghanistan and transferred to MacDill Air force Base in Tampa Florida. She continued working for Demetri's organization in Florida. Her position in Military Intelligence allowed her to supply information for the organizations ships that smuggled large caches of heroine from overseas, avoiding drug detection and interdiction by the Coast Guard in the waters off Florida. The money was good for the information she supplied to the Russian criminals, but it was not enough for the risk. Life in Prison was worth more then she was paid. Plainly she wanted more money. She had contacted Demetri and made it clear, more money and immediately or he would regret it.

Robert was upset with Dawn about her new demands. Dawns was pretty and tonight she looked especially thrilling in her short dress, but her problem was she really thought she wasn't expendable. He spoke to the point,

"Why are you screwing around getting greedy with these people. They have paid you well and we should be able to leave the country within the year and never be found. We have lots of money."

"No Robert, I don't have enough for what I do for them. You're a jerk, they make millions in a month and I am entitled to more. You want to be a chump, go ahead. They'll pay, these people understand only one thing and that's strength. I have all the cards in my deck. My information makes what they do possible."

When Robert and Dawn arrived at "Chubby's" dance and drink club, Boris waved them over to a booth.

"Hello my fine American friend, sit drink some vodka and tell me your cares." Boris wondered if Captain Sherman would also become dissatisfied with the money he was being paid by the organization.

Dawn ordered a glass of wine and Robert a beer. Boris sat across from Robert and Dawn in the booth with two of his Serbian body guards. He liked the looks of the pretty Lieutenant and wished he could spend some private time with her, maybe get her to reconsider. Her information helped with the operations, the smuggling was key to take over of the drug trade in the city of Tampa. To bad his orders from Demetri were final, no negotiation.

Boris gulped his vodka down and ordered another, looked at the two Americans and thought of how naïve they really were. They were traitors to the American dream, the American military, in Russia they would have been sent to Siberia and shot.

Boris began, "so you I am told you want more money. You have been paid many dollars, We have been good to you since Savvy makes deal with you. But now you tell me you will hurt me, my boss Demetri, and cause us problems. How much more do you want?"

Dawn felt empowered, Boris had asked her how much more she wanted, he wanted to negotiate, these Russian men were just muscled buffoons in expensive suits.

Richard Schmidt

Dawn spoke fast "I want five million in my account, I have delivered a lot to you and I have thought about selling my information to your competitors, who would pay me handsomely."

Boris smiled and said "Yes your information to our competitors would create problems. So you will have the money, and you, Robert Sherman do you to demand more money?"

Sherman shook his head no and said, "I am fine with our arraignment, she doesn't speak for me"

"Well then everybody is happy," Boris picked up his drink and said, "Drink with Boris and please enjoy life."

After several drinks, Dawn got up to use the ladies room Boris nodded to his two Serbian body guards and they followed Dawn and grabbed her with lighting speed, and hustled her into the kitchen of the club and out the back door. It happened so fast, she was slow from too much alcohol, once outside she was slugged in the head and pushed into a van. A rough looking man slammed the van door. She was aware of what was happening and tried to fight back scratching the man's face. He stumbled and she turned towards the door to escape. He pulled a .45 pistol from his waist, the muzzle wrapped with a dirty

30

towel to muffle the sound. He fired a single shot her into her head killing her instantly.

The two body guards watched as the van drove off. They returned to the table and told Boris in Russian "It has been done. The bitch is dead."

Boris smiled and said to Robert, "I have a new job for you. You will be paid handsomely for your services. You will pick a man up in the bay with your boat and bring him to your quarters. He will stay with you for a short time and you will assist him in getting around the city. This man is a professional. Boris handed him a paper with the particulars of when to pick the man up. Memorize the information and coordinants now and then burn it in the ash tray in front of me.

Robert memorized the information and gave Boris an account number for the money he would be paid to be deposited.

Boris looked at Robert and said "the girl will not be leaving with you she left the building with friends of mine."

The body of 1st Lt. Dawn Ross was found under the interstate off West Gandy Blvd. She had a bullet in the back of her head and her body lay in the dirt face down. A patrol officer found her about 3:00 a.m. when he was checking on the vagrants that congregated under the road drinking the beer under the over pass. A small wallet in her jeans pocket contained various credit cards a military I.D. and a California Driver's License that identified who she was. Her white turtle neck sweater was stained red from the large bullet hole in her head dripping blood. She smelled of perfume and death. She had a silver chain around her neck, holding her military dog tags in the rubber case. Homicide Detective Harry Smith was on call and responded to the scene. He checked the victim's gunshot wound and directed Crime Scene Technicians to collect trace evidence on her clothes, hair and body. Scrapings under her fingernails were taken for D.N.A. The technicians scoured the immediate area for anything that might help solve this affair. Smith had twenty plus years on the job and was looking to retire. He was burned out and had become dependent on whiskey and Coke to sleep each night. Another murder victim, another tragedy, another statistic of crime war and this one, a pretty girl. Smith figured this was a case of a jealous lover pissed off at his squeeze. He bent down over the body and noticed the military dog tags and I.D. He looked up at the patrol officer and said, "This one's not a regular she's an officer from the base. This is going to make the papers."

Smith shook his head. She wasn't some ugly street whore, alcoholic, or a homeless Jane Doe with no teeth. This crime scene led the Detective Smith to believe a pissed off boyfriend or girlfriend had decided if they couldn't have her nobody could. This was a slam dunk, solved time to file a report get some overtime and go home for a cold beverage. Harry Smith would be most expedient, he would let the Air force investigation services find him a suspect from the base, somebody she was sleeping with. Lean on them in an interrogation and get a confession. After all she was a government problem and Harry didn't want to miss his weekly golf game doing police work on a day off. Harry wanted to keep a low profile close his cases without too much work stress and coast into retirement. Smith called MacDill Airforce Base and spoke with the Base Police Desk Sergeant.

Smith identified himself to the Desk Sergeant who verified a Lieutenant Dawn Ross was stationed and lived on MacDill. Smith made a note of the address and told him, "you guys will have one less assigned in the morning, we found her murdered." The Sergeant hesitated for a second and said, "O.K. I'll notify the Base Commander and her Squadron Commander. We will have mortuary affairs make arrangements to claim her, when you are ready to release the body. Good night sir."

CHAPTER - 4

Air force OSI agent Jeff Brightwater of MacDill Air Force Base Tampa Florida was notified of the murder of Lieutenant Dawn Ross. He checked her record and found that she was assigned to the 66th military intelligence squadron. Prior to the 66th, she had served in a military intelligence unit in Afghanistan. She reviewed and analyzed all Intel from drones and communications that were intercepted. He called her squadron commander to see what he knew about the Lieutenant.

Major Jenkins her squadron commander was very shocked over the news about Ross, he told Brightwater "I just can't believe this has happened, I just saw her yesterday at our daily briefing."

"Major were you familiar with her activities or who she befriended on or off base" asked Brightwater.

"Yes, she attended the typical officer functions at the officers club. I didn't know of any relationships. I know she liked to workout at the gym when she wasn't here on duty. She was a private person, didn't say too much. She did talk to me about her plans to take leave in Europe and planned to visit her family in Los Angeles in the spring. She told me about her first assignment after she graduated officers training going to Afghanistan, she was an efficient officer, wanted to make a career of the of the Air force, I just can't believe this terrible thing has happened to her "the Majors voice became quiet and Bridgewater continued with his question,

"Yes sir, I see she has a top secret clearance".

Jenkins sighed and said "yes she was cleared to see and work on top priority intelligence information this section gathers."

"Major, I want to take a look at her work area and desk, I'll confiscate the computers and speak with her squadron members", Bridgewater spoke with his O.S.I. authority "That all for now Major, if I have any further questions 'll call you. Thank you."

Brightwater drove to her residence on base and used a pass key to get in. The place was neat and clean. He searched her desk and bureau in her bedroom. He smelled a sweet perfume in her bathroom and found a key to a safety deposit box in a red paper holder with the logo from a local credit union. There were study manuals from her squadron and books on politics and a book on diamonds and stones at her bedside table. A large screen T.V. was hanging on the wall in the living room and he noticed a set of speakers and an IPOD by her laptop on the kitchen counter. He found no pictures of any significant others. Dawn Ross appeared to be married to the Air Force. He pocketed the key to her bank box. He would make a check of it. He took her personal computer from a desk in the living room and placed it in a bag after he tagged it, he would review the files. Agent Bridgewater was done here, a feeling of sadness passed over him for this young life that was now no longer in the smart base apartment. He would ensure mortuary affairs forward the rest of her property to her family. He shut and locked the door.

The Tampa Coroner completed its autopsy of Lt. Ross. The Air Force shipped her body to her family in Los Angeles California for burial. Brightwaters' investigation of the Lieutenant on the air base was fruitless. Dawn Ross was a loner, she kept a low profile and stayed to herself. He checked with Tampa P.D. and they had no suspects in her murder off base. He hoped her personal computer files would shed some light on her.

Captain Robert Sherman was eating a protein filled breakfast, when he heard the local talk radio station report the murder of Lt. Ross. Sherman felt a chill go down his back. Sherman was still in disbelief that Ross had made such a stupid move, to try and black mail the Russians. He would never get greedy with these people. He finished his breakfast, showered, dressed and left his base apartment. He drove his cherry red Mustang GT to the base marina and boarded his 45 foot cabin cruiser with an 860 horsepower engine that cruised with ease into the waters of western Florida. He cast off the ropes tied to the dock and began his journey into the Gulf of Mexico. The thought of the money he was being paid was intoxicating. Robert Sherman would soon be living in a foreign country with his new wealth. No more would he take orders from the robots in the Pentagon who has sold out to the socialist politicians who were running the country into the fires of hell. These men who had never served a day in their life in the military, but who started wars for money, sacrificed good young men's lives for their gain. Sherman thought about his service to his country and became angry. The United States would leave Afghanistan without victory, without providing the Afghan people with anything but another corrupt master.

Even his own father a retired General, would never question the insane policies of the puppet masters in the Pentagon. It would never end the people would continue to buy into the lies about Afghanistan being a threat to America. The war was a no win situation the way the military had been directed to fight. Not Robert Sherman, no more wars for him, he would be wealthy and disappear to live a rich man's life far away from the United States. He would become a traitor, a criminal, no an opportunist. Yes just like the business men and lawyers who stole the people's money every day in the banks and the stock market, he would be an opportunist. Robert told himself he was just making a living, and why not a twenty year pension was not enough to live the kind of life he wanted.

The base water way was only open to boats from the base. The Coast Guard Commanders knew Captain Sherman's from the base officers club and always allowed him the professional courtesy of never stopping or boarding his boat for inspection. Sherman smelled the gulf water and shed his shirt receiving the beautiful sun rays on his already tan skin. He monitored his VHS radio and followed his GPS coordinates he had memorized form the paper Boris had given him. Ross spied the ship, it flew a Panamanian flag. Radio contact was made and Ross directed his boat to his coordinates and the divers appeared from under the choppy water.

CHAPTER - 5

Tampa Chief of Police Jennifer Ortiz sat proudly at her desk. Jennifer Ortiz was the progressive face of the new Tampa Police Dept. She had been a recruited and hired three years before from Seattle Washington, where she had started her career in the King County Sheriff's Office rising to the rank of Major. She commanded the Corrections Section, Patrol, and Criminal intelligence and then was appointed as the Chief Deputy for the Department. Ortiz was a master administrator and her job performance was renowned. Her performance led to a national reputation, as a reformer, helping to lead the King's County Sheriff's Department into the modern world. She was a solid crime fighter who the community respected and supported. When the Mayor of Tampa presented to her the opportunity for the job as Chief of Police in Tampa Florida, there was never a doubt in her mind, it was her destiny. Ortiz, who was bilingual, and ran five miles daily. She accepted the job in Tampa and never looked back. In Tampa she was known to show up in the middle of the night on a call to observe her officers and didn't have any aversion to getting involved to help an officer make an arrest in the field. She was by all means in charge.

Lt. Burns was summoned to the Chiefs Office by her personal aid Sergeant Adrian Ross. The Chief, seated at her desk, was always prepared to get right to the business at hand. She looked at Burns and said

"Lieutenant Burns, hoped you enjoyed your vacation last week, I will get right to the reason you're here. There was a homicide last week. A female Lieutenant from MacDill was found murdered under the Gandy overpass. I am assigning your unit to take this one from homicide and work it. I have notified the Homicide Commander, Major Beckett you will be taking the case and he is to give you any assistance you request. The Mayor called me and is concerned that this type of crime and the circumstances has caused an alarm for the military folks from the base. I don't want to bore you with the money the base and personal provide for Tampa's economy or the fact the press coverage this type of violent crime in Tampa garners. Homicide has a enough of a case load therefore, I want you to take this particular case and give your undivided attention to its closing. I want to close this one as soon as you can. Your unit is adapt, to resolving anything thrown its way and I see no reason why this should be any different."

Dan's reply was quick and to the point, "I'll give it a good look Chief, and see what we can turn up and hope to get an arrest."

"Good Lt, I also saw you report on the Gardens bust. Heroin from Afghanistan, Eastern Europeans being picked up in the raid, looks like the Russian mob has moved in."

"We have a bartender working as an informant in the Blue Fog and he has reported the owner had some outstanding debt, drugs and gambling losses. About a month ago he had a visit from a group of gentlemen that drank all the vodka in the place and had Russian accents. Bartender said the owner signed the place over to them for as payment. So yeah I'd say there here. Rumor from the street is the Russians have come up from Miami. They are working the area and have been pushing their dope, prostitution, protection rackets and all around bullshit on everybody."

"What about the local mob people, have they confronted the Russians or made any moves yet?" She pushed her chair back to become more comfortable and waited for an answer.

"No Chief, the locals are unorganized and have been depleted by all the years of the Feds locking them up on R.I.C.O. They rely on a small drug trade, identity theft, some gambling, prostitution and loan sharking that's keeping them afloat. The Mexican Cartels have also cut into the locals business. They have taken over a lot of the action, their people dealing and supplying dope to the state. It appears the Russians want to contend and push everybody else out. Another player in the dope game, to our fair city. That's seventy five cent story. The raid on the Gardens drug house was Afghan heroine which the Russians smuggled here."

"Yes, Afghan heroine is powerful stuff, we need to fine its source quick and stop those responsible or we could have an epidemic of junkies in the city. The cheap Mexican product is bad enough but not as powerful. The cartels shipping cocaine from Mexico won't be happy to find out the Russians are invading their market. Let's hope we don't have a war between the parties jockeying for first place. Alright then, keep an eye on the locals, the Cartel and our Russian friends." Chief Ortiz looked at

Dan and spoke sternly, "Dan deal with this case of the dead MacDill Lieutenant quickly. It's something we need to put to rest."

Dan looked at her and nodded. He left her office with some reservations. His experience told him if you work to quick you miss important things, things that could be deadly in so many ways.

Sergeant Ross watched Dan leave and admired his cool approach. She asked the Chief,

"Do you think he will resolve this quickly?"

Ortiz shot her a smile and said "Let's hope so. He's a believer in right and wrong, justice and people, a man who has kept his idealism, which allows him to cope with what he sees every day. I believe that's what keeps him above all the madness.

Chapter - 6

Captain Sherman spoke with the two divers briefly. They were Russian, former Spetnaz commandos. The bigger of the two men changed in the cabin with clothes and shoes carried in a water proof bag he brought aboard. The other diver's waterproof bag was opened and contained a Russian sniper rifle and a police pistol with a couple of boxes of ammo. A small sealed metal box was also in the waterproof bag. The box, weapons and ammo where transferred into a green duffel bag Sherman had brought onto the boat. For this smuggling, a cool one million dollars was deposited into Sherman's Caymans island bank account. The smaller of the two divers, gave a nod to the other and went back overboard, disappearing into the water, headed back to the ship.

Sherman explained firmly to his new crew member

"When we arrive back at the base beach say nothing to anyone and stay with me as if we are friends returning from a day of boating."

The man smiled and waved his hand in a mocking gesture toward Sherman. He was well muscled and the clothes fit his hard frame tight. He answered Sherman in perfect English, with the hint of a Russian accent, "I have a passport in the name Thomas Gold, when we get to your base I am to stay hidden in your quarters until I am contacted. You are to give me any assistance I need. You have been paid well; you know what is expected of you."

Sherman was seated at the wheel of the boat sizing up Thomas Gold, who stood next to him and picked up the pistol from the bag, looked at Sherman and placed the pistol back into the bag. Sherman knew there was no turning back now. He thought about the money. He turned the big engine on and pushed the throttle forward heading the boat for the base beach and dock. The return trip was free of any coast guard cutters and when they arrived at the base beach the Russian laughed at the lack of any security to stop or check the boat. It was late at night and the base beach was quite and vacant. The two men tied the boat up at the dock grabbed the duffle bag and went to Sherman's car in the parking lot. A base security police vehicle passed them as they drove on the Airbases main drag on the way to Sherman's quarters. Then Russian laughed and said to Sherman "You Americans are so trusting they never would think a man could be smuggled into a military installation. Your borders are a joke. Americans are so naïve and trusting, that is why the world detest you."

They arrived at Sherman's quarters and the Russian immediately went to Sherman's bar and poured double shot of vodka. He used a phone Sherman had been supplied for him and called a number he had memorized. Speaking Russian, to prevent Sherman from knowing what his orders were, he wrote an address down hung the phone up, looked at Sherman and said "Now my friend, I rest for some time and we then continue our operation."

Dan asked Mike Hanson his squad Sergeant to meet him at the office after his meeting with the Chief and explained to him the task at hand. Mike was African American; his shirts were tailored and fit tight to his large frame. He was always squared away, He had played professional football for a few years in Tampa and when his football career was over and wanting to stay in Tampa, he became a Tampa cop. Mike Hanson could intimidate anybody with his physical size, but he never had to because Mike could out think most. He had an I.Q. of one hundred and seventy. Jeopardy was no contest his mind was a computer on steroids.

"Mike we have a directive from Chief Ortiz to take over a homicide case and work it. The Mayor is putting pressure on the Chief to put this one in the solved file yesterday, so the citizens and military members won't worry about safety in our fair city. I want you to beat the bushes on this one. Do what you do best, and find the killer."

Hanson sipped his stale warm coffee and replied with a grin, "I need the overtime Football tickets are so expensive on this salary, besides my mortgage and can't forget my car payment."

Dan poured a cup of coffee from the office pot and briefed Hanson on the particulars of the murder up to the present.

"Patrol found the young Air force Lieutenant under the Gandy overpass, with a gunshot to the back of the head. "Harry Smith was the detective on call, and arrived to the scene to investigate. Smith feels it's a lover's quarrel with a bad ending, of course Harry Smith pitched the easiest motive, with no real investigation, find a boyfriend or girlfriend, get a confession and its closed. He's been retired on duty for the last five years so he wasn't going to be creative, too much work. So he came up empty. Nothing on file as for domestic trouble for her, no boyfriend that is known, you're going to have to see if the streets have anything that will lead us to a motive. Her killer may be on the Airbase. The chief is concerned that our friends in city hall will get a backlash from the brass at MacDill if we don't find her killer within a reasonable amount of time. I want you to start with her family in L.A. Speak with her parents, get a background from before she went into service and if there is anything from her past that may have resurfaced. The Airforce will give us only the sanitized version of her career, great officer so forth. Get in contact with O.S.I. on the base, and talk to them see if we can go on base and look in her quarters. They should have no problem with that. I'm sure the O.S.I. has looked at her activity on the base to see if she had any problems. The report from the autopsy shows a single shot to the back of the head. Body had some trace D.N.A. evidence on it. No match yet. Her purse and contents are in evidence, Stay in touch."

Mike Hanson contacted Air force Special Agent Dennis Brightwater who was assigned by the Air force, to give any assistance to the local authorities on the Ross investigation. Hanson met with him at a local coffee shop right outside of the Airbase. Hanson ordered breakfast for the both of them. Brightwater watched as Mike devoured the plate of eggs, bacon, and toast and finished the coffee. Bridgewater recognized Hanson the former pro football linebacker and was thrilled to be in his company.

Hanson pushed his plate aside and looked into Brightwaters eyes. Hanson liked what he saw, honesty, this dude was straight up, and he could feel a good vibration. Brightwater was just a nice guy.

"Where you from Brightwater, you got to be from the west!!"

"South Dakota, a small town called Redfield. A place where a man farms to make a living. Cold winters and short hot summers." Brightwater smiled as he finished.

Hanson began "I've read the case file and looked at the small amount of evidence we have on the victim Lt. Ross and it looks to me that she pissed in somebodies cornflakes. She took a shot to the back of the head with a 45 automatic slug. Nasty way to go out, besides being left under a freeway. That's just not right. Was she known to you or your office?"

Hanson sipped his coffee and placed the cup down on the table waiting for the answer. "No, she had no known disciplinary problems, fast track on her career, young and pretty, going places. I've done a search of her apartment and had her work and personal computer sent to search the hard drives. I found a key to a safety deposit box which I have yet to open. She had no real friends on base, kept everything real professional with everyone, a bit of a loner.

Hanson tapped his fingers on the table and looked at Brightwater and said, I spoke to her mother by phone, she's in L.A. was devastated about her murder. Mother had no information on her daughter personal life far as she knew there was no significant other, said she last saw her before she left for Afghanistan. Sounds like she was a recruiting add. Beautiful, smart, career minded and no skeletons or know vices. Just can't be, everybody has something you just got to find it."

Brightwater replied with enthusiasm "Let get started." Hanson smiled, he knew he had broken the ice with Brightwater and they would work well together.

Dirty Mike McGee parked his Harley and entered the club house of Satan's Wolves on Florida Avenue. He looked across the street and saw the white van parked, he knew they were cops filming the club house for who came and went. Probably locals maybe the Feds. The thought of the cops and there surveillance bullshit made him angry. McGee had been in there jails and prisons and done his time. When he finished his time the only family he had were Satan's Wolves. His life was the Motorcycle club and he hated society, its rules and most of all, cops. Cops were parasites who tried to infiltrate the clubs and create chaos for the brothers. Not in Satan's Wolves, everybody was tight and you had to prospect with some passion to become a member. Times were good, the drug business was booming, everybody wanted to get high and Dirty Mike was a natural money maker. He and the club were also was now contracting loan shark enforcement for the mobs. Drug dealing was the main earner for Dirty Mike and the club members. Dirty Mike also supplied girls to the topless bars that the mob owned in Tampa. Finding them was so easy; turning them out was all in a day's work. The new guys on the block, the Russians were also using Dirty Mikes talents and he had done a few hard core jobs for them. They meant business, you did your job for them, no bullshit, they didn't play, fuck with them and they wouldn't hesitate to kill you. The bitch he iced for them, tried to fight, but he finished her with one shot. The job complete, he dumped her body under an overpass. The Russian paid him in green and threw in some dope, he would always know Dirty Mike was the man to use.

Detectives Denise Ramstein and Bill Barton sat in their unmarked car and watched Dirty Mike enter the door of the Biker club house. They were assigned by Lt. Burns to keep an eye on the bikers club house to see who came and went. The heroin bust in the Gardens had netted one of the Biker gang members and S.I.U. wanted to know what the gangs ties were to the dope. Information from street informants, was the bikers were doing contract work for the Russians. They recognized Dirty Mike wearing his vest with the club rocker. Surveillance on the club in the past by S.I.U. had identified Dirty Mike as a club officer who had a long arrest sheet.

Ramstein and Barton had nothing in common other then they worked together as partners. Denise Ramstein was a beautiful burnet who had been a cop for the last ten years. She was an intense person. Denise had two rules in life do the right thing and be responsible. Living by the two rules every day, made all her decisions simple. She was a college educated, single mother, and her ten year old son was her world. Her one and only husband an accountant had died several years before, suddenly of an aneurism. Denise had to find a career to support herself and her son. Denise pursued being a police officer and after a lot of hard work she became a Tampa Cop. She ran five miles a day and lifted weights to keep in shape, and deal with the stress of her career.

Bill Barton was a twenty year veteran, lived by himself, smoked a pack of cigarettes a day ate nothing but spicy food, and his life was his job. Bill and Denise made good partners because they both loved the job. They got along, but were as different as night and day. Bill sipped his cold coffee in between snapping pictures of the bikers coming and going.

Denise made small talk "Bill, you seen any good movies lately?"

"Nah, just watching a lot of T.V. reality shows, How's your kid doing?"

"To smart for his own good, hey that white van across the street what's up with that" Denise replied while picking up the radio mic"

"Seventeen Indigo to Central can you have any surveillance units on 156th street and Florida Ave identify itself over. Central to any unit on 15th Street and Florida Ave respond with your call sign over. Central to Seventeen Indigo no unit responds, over.

"Seventeen Indigo, copy. Who do we have over there Bill" asked Denise.

"Got to be the Feds snooping around maybe looking to make a R.I.C.O. case" I'll get with intelligence and see if they know who's looking at these fine young men", said Barton with his dry sarcasm.

Nick Hanson and another man who was a professional assassin sat in the white van watching the club house. They were waiting for Dirty Mike and saw the cops. Nick Hanson C.I.A. agent was in town working for the mysterious "Mr. Jones". Nick loved money and he was paid handsomely by a group of private people in Europe to do "odd" jobs for them.

Lt. Dan Burns entered the county jail and requested the Deputy at the front desk call for an inmate on the 5th floor of the jail named Bobby Dobbins. Dobbins was escorted to the interview room and placed into the room. Dan entered the room and both men shook hands. Bobby Dobbins was now a criminal who has been in and out of jail over the last three years due to a bad addiction to cocaine. Before that Bobby had been a police officer for the city of Tampa. Bobby had been on drug task force and was in a shooting and killed a fourteen year old boy who had pointed a gun at him during a raid on a drug house. Dan had investigated the shooting for the Chief and with the State Attorney investigators they found that Bobby had been justified in his shooting the teen. Bobby was never the same after the shooting; he began drinking then using cocaine and heroin to deal with his guilt in the death of the young criminal. Eventually the department had to fire him as he was unable to function as a reasonable human being let along a Police Officer. Dan attempted to offer Bobby help but he would never stop destroying himself. When in jail he would get sober and call Dan with information he heard from other inmates in the jail. Bobby was not a snitch, or an informer, he was in his own way still trying to be a Police Officer, trying to make up for his mistake, the child he shot and killed. It would never bring the child back, but the more scum he helped put away the more the child of the streets were safe from them. Dan would come and put money in his jail account for commissary items, while he was locked up for his possession charges, which occurred many times. His information was always good and Dan hoped he would somehow stay clean when he was released back to the street, but Bobby always fell prey to his habit.

"Bobby I will get right to the point, I need you to put out your feelers, I have a young women who was an Air force Officer, shot dead and found under an underpass.

Not much to go on. I need a lead. The jail occupants talk a lot, information floating around, so if you hear anything concrete, call me and I will talk to the State about this charge they have on you."

Bobby had a surge go through his body he was needed again, he felt useful. He could help he wanted to help because he wanted to get better and he had to feel good about himself again. He was after all a sick person, a doper, a lost soul, but he had been a cop and a good one, just maybe he could provide the answer Dan needed. Finding the girls killer would give him a spark, his life a goal, some purpose, get him out of the desperate world of addiction he was a prisoner in. Killing him with the heroin he used. The heroin was the only thing that helped the pain brought on by, consistently seeing the child fall from the bullet he shot with his gun.

The prospect of solving a case, helping catch a killer, gave Bobby a lift and he said with enthusiasm "No problem I'll get you some answers, jail house is full of talk all the time, I hear anything you'll be the first to know."

"O.K. Bobby, I put some money in your account, and I will talk to the State about you. Do you think you would be open to treatment again?" Dan asked.

Bobby looked at Dan and said "If I don't get clean I know the devil will take me to his house."

Dennis Brightwater and Mike Hanson opened the safe deposit box and found a computer disk and fifty thousand dollars in cash. Bridgewater pulled his computer out of the carrying case and uploaded it. The disk contained the schedule of the ships coming to the port of Tampa from Ports in Europe via the Panama Canal for the last six months. A Classified list of Coast Guard cutters, their Captains, crews and their duty routes in Florida waters were also listed. Computer programs for Radio frequencies and a list of the names of port managers in Europe and the Panama Canal. There disk was titled "Bratvia".

Brightwater reading the P.C. screen looked at Hanson and quietly said, "Appears the Lieutenant was involved selling information."

Hanson sneered, "Yeah. She has a boat load of money, no pun intended and I bet yeah she never called the I.R.S. to report this lute."

"The Air force will be interested in who she was involved with......, and the money?" Brightwater fell silent and looked at Hanson.

Hanson said in his logical way "Criminal act, you're the military, you can grab the green stuff now, due to national security or something along those bureaucratic lines. You'll be busy with the implications, what harm has been done to the country an so on. I on the other hand still have a murder to solve but this gives me a road to follow." Hanson smiled

Brightwater felt a bit overwhelmed, he told Hanson, "The Airforce is not going to be flying into the wild blue yonder on this one."

CHAPTER - 7

Salvador Hernandez and Carlos Gomez met in a Cuban coffee shop on Dale Mabry. Both men were the leaders of the two largest criminal organizations on the west coast of Florida. For years they had kept the city divided and all to themselves. The Italians who had at one time ruled the city had all but lost their power to the Hernandez and Gomez organizations. They kept the business of loan sharking, prostitution and drug dealing profitable, all the while staying one step from the authorities. They had close ties with the Mexican Cartels and imported the Cartels drugs. They were insulated by legitimate businesses they used to launder their criminal profits. They paid the best criminal lawyers to keep them out of jail. The men and women who worked for them knew if they were busted they might have to do time, but their families would be taken care of by the organization, and beside if they snitched on Salvador or Carlos no place would be safe for them. The crime lords had connections in the Police and the Court house.

The two shook hands and exchanged pleasantries. The meeting was to discuss the Russians, sudden takeover of several bars and clubs and who were selling their dope in the territories the two men controlled.

A large man came out from the kitchen, and asked the men what they would care to drink. Salvador told the man to bring them each a cup of Cuban coffee. The man nodded his head and headed for the kitchen. Once in the kitchen, the man opened a small box the one he had brought with him when he had boarded Captain Sherman's boat and took from the box a liquid vile and poured the substance into the cups of Cuban coffee. Placing the filled coffee cups on a tray, he walked out of the kitchen to the men's table and served them the beverage.

Carlos the more excitable of the two finished his cup of coffee and began to rant, "These bastards have been causing problems for my people, even gone so dam far as to attack my street dealers, they have been buying up clubs, pushing my people out, and bringing in women from their country to dance and turn tricks. I am losing money, people and territory. This has to stop. I will burn them for this, I will go to war and I need you to go to war with me.!"

Salvador drained his cup and placed his hand in front of Carlos to quiet his tirade. He looked at Carlos and said in calm voice "My friend we own the city, these people have come to our streets and have tried to take want is ours. We will deal with them my friend and we will do it soon, but we must be careful to act with strength when the time is right, Carlos remember we will be the masters of our fate."

The Russian walked up to the table and asked both men if they would like another cup of coffee. Carlos tried to place the waiter's accent but was not sure where he was from. He looked at him and waved him away. Within a few minutes both crime bosses felt a burning sensation in their stomach, they both began to feel sweat roll off their faces and breathing became impossible. The waiter smiled at them and they attempted to get up but fell down without being able to break the fall. Carlos and Salvador were laying in their vomit, they were dead.

The Russian looked down at the two dead bodies and smiled. He went into the kitchen, past the dead owner of the shop who he had also killed.

Dan heard the Signal -5 come over the radio after the responding patrol office notified dispatch and arrived at the crime scene. A customer walked into the coffee shop for a midmorning pick me up and found the bodies and called police. Two men been found dead in the dining area and the proprietor shot dead in the kitchen. Dan recognized the two gangsters. They had met a bad ending, and Dan wondered how fast it would be before the retaliation hit the streets of Tampa. This act was the start of an organized crime turf war, and Tampa was the target.

"Lt. Burns what brings S.I.U. to this scene" asked the lead Homicide detective.

Dan smiled at the detective, looked at the two bodies, shook his head and asked, "Any witnesses"?

The detective, a veteran from Homicide, knew Burns was a fast rising star in the department.

"None yet, poison was used, look at the mouths of these two, a film on the lips, a toxic odor, vomit smells with the same odor. I've seen a few in my time but this stuff… killed them within minutes of ingestion. Until an autopsy is done I'm guessing this is something you don't get over the counter."

Dan had seen poison used while he was in the C.I.A. He remembered the Israelis using poison, instead of a remote control bomb, or a shooter team, against a Hamas target in a European city.

Dan went back to his car and contacted his Corporal Jack Bradley, who handled S.I.U. administrative duties for the squad.

Dan dialed Bradley's office phone "Jack call a staff meeting for the squad, tomorrow morning. I'm just leaving a signal 5 and both victims are Tampa mafia."

CHAPTER - 8

The Russian known as Thomas Gold was back in the base quarters of Captain Sherman. Sherman had driven the Russian to the coffee shop and waited in the car a block away as he was instructed to by the hit man. The Russian made a call on the throw away phone he had been provided and informed Boris, the plan was a success.

Boris immediately called Demetri and advised him of the success of their assassin.

Demetri drained his vodka glass and felt the Florida sun tan his burley body. He refilled his glass with more of the clear Russian vodka and began to bark orders at Boris.

"Take the streets over, send our people out now to grab the territory of these dead men. Tell their people we are in charge now, kill any of them who try and stop us. Flood the streets with our dope and undercut the price for a short time to ensure we have our product everywhere in the city. Any clubs they owned make them pay protection money or we will put them out of business. Boris we will meet later, the Blue Wave club for celebration."

"Of course Demetri, we will celebrate. I will drink good vodka, with many women tonight. The Police have nothing yet. But we must be careful. They will begin to look our way, so we must stay in the shadows."

"My friend Boris, you worry like old women on the farm. We still have our source to alert us of any new information. Bring in more of our people in the next week. Use the Air force Captain and his boat again, but be careful."

During the next two nights Captain Sherman and the Russian took Sherman's boat and rendezvoused with three more men from the freighters in the Gulf outside the base waterway and brought them on to the base beach in the late of night. They stayed in Captain Sherman's quarters till morning, and then Sherman would drive them to the house of Demetri.

It appeared that no one saw anything as Sherman and the Russians were careful to be stealth, they thought. A base Security Police patrol was parked in the shadows of the base beach and the young military cop Airman Tim Johnson watched as the men tied the boat to the on the second night. He thought the three men were back from a long night of fishing. But he never saw a fishing pole or tackle box, just a large bag one of the men carried as they got into a cherry red mustang, he had seen the car a few times on base a while working main gate control and who could forget seeing the really beautiful female Lieutenant in the passenger seat leaving the base not long ago. He wished he had the life of the officer who was driving a boss car, seen with a beautiful chick in the car, now coming in from a night on the water, in an awesome boat. Life sucked to be an enlisted man. He wished his shift was over, he was tired and hungry.

The S.I.U. squad meeting was at the downtown Hyatt Hotel in business meeting room where breakfast was served first. Dan wanted to review the cases they were working on, get the Dawn Ross case up to speed and update the squad on the mafia murders. Dan knew the murders of the two mob leaders by the Russian mobsters, was their move to gain control of the city.

Each member ate a hearty breakfast made small talk and finished their coffee. Hotel staff cleared the tables and left the room. Dan stated by briefing the squad about the Ross killing and the Chiefs desire for S.I.U. to solve the case. Dan asked Mike Hanson to give an update of the information he had gathered in the last couple of days.

Hanson cleared his throat and began

"The information I have gathered, leads me to conclude Lt. Ross was being paid to sell information. She had a hefty amount of cash in a safety deposit box and a disk with information on Coast Guard Patrol locations and shipping routes into Tampa Bay and its Port for ships coming in from overseas. The disk was marked "Bravita" which is Russian for Brotherhood. She was an Air force Intelligence specialist, so she had access to a treasure trove of information on government computers. Brightwater, the O.S.I. agent I'm working with, is checking her work and personal computers out, so I should have more goodies to share with you soon."

"Thanks Mike. OK Johnny... Ron anything on all that Afghan Heroin" asked Dan

Johnny Creasy spoke first; "the dope was pure Afghan heroin worth more than the city budget. The guys arrested at the Gardens were two Serbians, here on temporary Visas. Interpol was notified and they report both of them were known as drug runners and smugglers for the Russian Mob in Serbia. The third guy was a biker, member of Satan's Wolves, Criminal Intelligence has a file on him, been locked up a lot, says he's an old hand at cutting, cooking, and packaging dope.

Ron Becker added, "It looks like the owners of the dope are eastern Europeans, Narco said the A.K.'s confiscated in Gardens dope raid were Russian. Also word on the street is the Russians are making a move to take over the city. Criminal intelligence confirms a Russian organized crime family has moved into our fair city of Tampa, they have been doing business in Miami. The top dog is a guy named Demetri Stanasolsky AKA the "Beast". He stays under the radar. Immigration sent some pictures they had on file and his criminal history from Russia and Europe. We requested Miami P.D send us anything they have on him. His occupation is listed as a Baker but I don't think he's working nine to five making rolls. The Russian Government has not been cooperative with sharing information about him or his associates. Several strip clubs in town have new ownership and they now serve caviar and Russian vodka. Mafia from Moscow written all over this."

Corporal Jack Bradley spoke to the squad next," Hey we got a war going on, and the coffee shop hit was like some spy job. The M.E. says the cause of death was a poison called Polonium. Russian KGB agents used it on some poor guy, years ago in London.

Dan listened, turned to Denise and asked her a question.

"Denise what about the bikers, have they had any Russian guests at the club house or have they been selling there "old ladies" to the new Russian bar owners?"

Denise put her coffee cup down on the table and spoke to the group "Word from informants is bars and clubs around town have an influx of new owners with girls from eastern Europe and some homegrown biker women from the area. Lots of prostitution going on. We did some surveillance on the Satan Wolves club house, since a known club member was collared at the Gardens raid, we found somebody else, watching the club house so we ran a check and it came up empty, wasn't the Sheriff, Florida Dept of Law Enforcement or the F.B.I. So put in a call to Criminal Intelligence, and they said you didn't hear it from them, but the word was a girlfriend of a guy in intel, works as an analyst for the F.B.I. downtown told him, C.I.A. people were in town and requesting F.B.I. information on Satan's Wolves."

Dan thanked Denise and said, "O.K. let's get back out in the field, get some more information on the Russian bosses, there agenda, and keep an eye on the biker gang Satan's Wolves. Let's not let them get too much of a foothold. I imagine the dope flooding the streets is coming directly into the port of Tampa and under the nose of the Coast Guard. Mike, the money you found in that deposit box, no doubt Russian payola for the work Lieutenant Ross was busy doing. The two murders in the coffee shop look to be a professional hit, my guess; the Russians eliminating the competition, letting everybody in town know there's a new comrade on the block."

Dan was not surprised to hear the C.I.A. may have been in town snooping around. His days working in the agency had brought him to Tampa a few times too. Tampa was a big city with a history of the criminal and intelligence world mixing together.

CHAPTER - 9

The Federal Building in Tampa was downtown. It was home to the Federal Courts and many Federal Agencies including the F.B.I. D.E.A. and the rest of the overstaffed Federal Agencies. The C.I.A. has an office in the building under a phony government cover, the Office of Federal Energy Control, but only a few privileged people had knowledge of this. The senior agent in charge was Nicholas Harmon. He had served the agency well, working posts in the Middle East, Europe, and was a master of interrogations at the secret prisons in various places in the underground world. Harmon was only interested in one thing and that was Nicolas Harmon. He was called Nick the prick, behind his back by all who worked with him. He hated everybody equally. Being a C.I.A. agent, Nick used power with malice; he had framed people, thrown them in secret prisons, and when necessary, killed whoever he felt was a threat. His use of agency assassins and, hunting then terminating targets, by the use of the drone was his specialty. National Security was Nicks catch all. If somebody needed to be killed Nick categorized them as a National Security threat. Nicholas Harmon answered only to high ranking superiors at the agency, and they loved his dirty ways. Money was also a very important part of Nicholas' life. Money opened doors. The government gave him plenty to spread around, grease the hands of those in high and low places to accomplish what Uncle Sam said was good foreign policy. Dan had worked with him in Paris. Dan never trusted Nick and was suspicious of him. Events Nick was involved in, with Dan in Paris took an almost deadly turn. Dan and Nick didn't like each other. Dan had knocked Nick on the floor with one punch, after coming to the aid of a women who was desperately trying to flee Nicks insulting, and rude behavior toward her at an embassy function. After Dan's attempt to correct Nick's behavior, Nick stormed making vague threats to Dan of getting even. Weeks later during an operation, Nick lied to Dan and left him to be bait for an international terrorist. Dan was tasked to meet an informer and pay him 10,000 Euros for information that would lead to a raid on a safe house set up in the Arrondissement neighborhood of Paris hiding Al-Qaida members. When the informer showed up so did a hit team of Al-Qaida. Who had tipped them off? Dan always figured it was Nick, who acted very surprised when Dan showed up unharmed at the American Embassy with the informant. Dan had eluded the hit team by using a stairway to a roof and a mad dash to safety. The informant told Dan he recognized Nick in past meetings with members of the Al-Qaida cell, but would say no more after demanding his money, a new identity and passage to the United States.

Dan watched Nick sipping coffee at the canteen reading a copy of the Tampa Times. Nicks cell phone rang and he engaged in a conversation, and abruptly left heading for the main entrance. Dan followed him staying back far enough to conceal himself. Nick left in a vehicle once on the interstate, after a few miles, he turned off for Davis Island. Dan pulled over to the side of the road and observed the grey Lexus SUV Nick drove and watched as he pulled into a driveway waited for the gates to open and disappeared behind the landscape. Dan pressed speed dial on his cell and Johnny Creasy answered "What's happening Boss, you cool?"

Johnny I've tailed a guy to 3548 Sea Breeze Street Davis Island and I want you to get in your vehicle and meet me down the block, asap.

"I'm on it boss, be there in a few", Johnny said moving to his car while checking his firearm.

When Johnny arrived he found Dan sitting in his car watching the house he had followed Nick to. Dan came right to the point when Johnny entered into Dan's car." There's a scumbag name Nick Harmon in that house. Blond hair, dark blue suit,. You can't miss him. I called the address in and the house belongs to a Reality company that's leasing it to the occupant. I want you to sit on the place and when this guy comes out stay on him and let me know his movements, and Johnny the guy is C.I.A. so he will be wise, if your sloppy with your tail. Don't make contact with him, he can be dangerous.

"Right on Boss, this guy is agency. Far out." Johnny smiled and laughed when he made the comment.

"Just track his movements and keep your cell phone handy. Alright Johnny cool, stay in touch. Stay off the radio, I want to keep this under the radar until we see what's going on with this guy."

Dan sped off, he had a meeting with the Chief of Police and she didn't like anyone to be late

CHAPTER - 10

Air force O.S.I. agent Jeff Brightwater sat in his Base office with a Staff Sergeant who was a forensic computer specialist, The Staff Sergeant, diligently dissected the hard drives of Lt. Ross' work and personal computers. The Sergeant gave Brightwater a print out of the files and information on them. The files spelled out the whole dirty mess of her complicity in a smuggling operation of heroin. The Air force was not going to be thrilled at explaining this and how she pulled this off under the noses of her superiors. Her personal computer was an accounting of the filthy money she had been paid along with someone she referred to "Sky Eagle". He was certain her murder was connected to her crime and now he had to find out who "Sky Eagle" was.

Dan entered the Chiefs office and was met by the Chiefs liaison Sergeant Adrian Ross. Ross was always professional looking, but she had a sexy edge. Dan exchanged pleasantries with her and took a seat on the couch in the office.

Chief Ortiz entered the office and asked, "Lt. Burns what progress have you made on the Ross murder investigation?"

"Chief, it appears our victim was dirty. There's a war going on in Tampa with the Russian mob eliminating the heads of the Gomez and Hernandez families. I think the death of the Lieutenant Ross may be tied to the Russians moving large amounts of drugs into the city, they have taken over various clubs and street operations. To make matters worse in this mess, the C.I.A. has been snooping around town and I don't believe in coincidences."

Ortiz tapped her fingers on the mahogany desk and looked at Dan. She remained calm and said to him,

"I don't want this to get any worse. Make an arrest on the murder of the Lieutenant as soon as you can, the mob fight over this city may be a blessing in disguise, they destroy each other and we pounce on the winner. I don't want the Feds anywhere near this; they will take the credit for our work and leave us to take a fall it we miss something. Contact Sergeant Ross for a scheduled meeting with me when you have made more progress on the murder of the girl."

Dan got up and left the chiefs office. When Dan left the chiefs office her secretary, Janis Carter a twenty year employee placed a call to a man named Boris. Janis' daughter was sick with a rare cancer. A man named Boris contacted Jane one night at her home and after offering her hope for her plight, paid all her daughters medical bills and had the best doctors in town treating the young girl just as long as Janis let Boris know of the things that went on in the Police Chiefs office.

Denise Ramstein and Bill Barton found Dirty Mike coming out of a strip club, he was known to frequent on Dale Mabry. They did a computer search on several of Satans Wolves and had found two outstanding traffic warrants Dirty Mike had for Failure to Appear in Court for Reckless Driving and Speeding. Denise walked up to him and flashed her badge. He tried to push past her but he stopped when she pushed back and pointed her police 45 pistol towards his chest, he threw his hands up and said "Fuckin bitch pig, what's the beef?"

Richard Schmidt

Denise informed him he was under arrest for a probation warrant in no uncertain terms and Barton placed him up against a car in the parking lot and snapped the cuffs on.

The arrest was police strategy, get the Biker into a cell with Bobby and see if he could get Dirty Mike to talk about why a club member was picked up in the Gardens Afghan heroin raid. The warrant was solid and would keep Dirty Mike in the can for at least a month before he could get a court hearing. Dirty Mike was the typical biker criminal who didn't think he had to pay his probation fines or report as scheduled. Dirty Mike was booked and processed. He had no bond and Denise notified a Deputy she knew in the jail criminal investigative unit and requested the biker be housed with Inmate Bobby Dobbins as directed by Lt. Burns.

Johnny Creasy watched as the gate to the house he was watching opened and three Cadillac S.U.V's rolled out into the street. The first vehicle stopped and waited in the road until both vehicles behind were in line. There were three men in the lead and trail vehicle and four men in the middle vehicle. The maneuver was military, keeping the middle vehicle guarded from the front and back. The convoy started to roll and headed for the interstate. Johnny stayed back, but followed the trail of cars without raising suspicion. He dialed Dan and advised him of his tail. As he spoke the caravan turned off to the port of Tampa.

"Lt. these fellas are heading for the port. They have some heavy looking muscle in the cars.

"Just bird dog am Johnny, keep them at a distance and gather what info you can. Get some pictures with your camera, I'm on my way."

Johnny slowed his car and followed them to the port gate where the gate guard waved them into the port area. They parked the vehicles in front of a warehouse The men piled out of the vehicles and went into the warehouse. Johnny flashed his badge and the gate guard waved him into the port complex. Johnny parked his car at the main gate parking and went to the personnel entry door of the warehouse and peeked inside staying undetected. He saw the men he had followed, now gathered with several Military officers in uniform. Johnny backed away and saw Dan had arrived. He went over to Dan's car and entered the passenger seat. Dan parked the car in a staff parking area so as not to be seen.

O.K. Boss there all here and you'll never guess who they are having tea with. There's Air force and Army brass in there with them and they seem to be in deep thought."

Dan thought for a second and asked "anything inside stand out other than them?"

"Nothing I saw other than a bunch of crates. Typical sailor shipping bullshit." Johnny liked the witty answer he gave.

Just then the men appeared leaving the warehouse. Johnny snapped his camera taking pictures of the party. Dan saw Nick and a big thick muscular man with greased jet black hair combed straight back. This had to be the Russian boss Demetri. Next to him was another man with the same greased hair but he was smaller. The Russians had body guards surrounding the group. The military officers appeared to be an army Major, and two full bird Colonels one Air force and one Army. There was an exchange of nods from the men and they went their separate ways. The Russians and Nick entered their vehicles and drove off. The military officers all left together in a Military staff car. Dan and Johnny went to the port security office. Dan identified himself to the security chief and under the guise of doing a Police inspection on a corrupt fire inspector he asked to enter the warehouse where the meeting between the Russians and the military officers had taken place. The Security Chief was very cooperating and led Dan and Johnny where they requested. The Security Chief made sure to tell Dan he "never liked the fire inspector and thought he was an overpaid pompous jackass."

When Dan entered the warehouse he looked at the crates and they were marked Aberdeen Proving Grounds U.S. Government property. The invoices read the crates had been shipped from the port of Baltimore and were marked destination MacDill Airforce Base. Dan Burns had no legal right to open the crates, nor be allowed to by the port officials without a search warrant. So he pulled off one of the invoices and put it in his coat pocket to a check run on it later. He would have to get a look at what was in the crates when no one was privy. The Russians, the military, the C.I.A., the murder the female officer, where was this going? Dan had a bad feeling, this was turning into a volcano that was about to erupt, and with an eruption always come devastation. Dan and Johnny thanked the chief and asked him to please tell no one of their visit.

CHAPTER - 11

Dirty Mike didn't mind jail it was just part of the life of a biker. He would catch up on his sleep and wait for a public pretended as he called the public defenders to get him a bond or a fine for his warrant on the traffic tickets and get back to the streets. There was another dude in the cell with him who was big and looked like he was able to take care of himself.

The jail was quiet and Dirty Mike looked at his Bunkie and said, "What the fuck dude, you know me."

Bobby looked at Dirty Mike, saw the biker gang tattoo's and didn't respond. Dirty Mike got up from the bunk and began to pace, "hey boy I'm talking to you, what's your fuckin problem you deaf or stupid?"

Bobby looked at him and said "I'm just tryin to give you a little respect, I know you and I like your style. I've seen you and your crew at the bars downtown. You guys ride hard and run the ladies. Keeps em in line."

Dirty Mike grinned and let out a burst of laughter. "I own them bitches. I run all them hoes. So you know, I'm the keeper of the house."

Bobby knew right away he had the attention of Mike by flattering him. He kept up the banter and the Biker became comfortable with the praise and the phony respect Bobby laid on the inflated ego of Dirty Mike. After a few more minutes of praising the biker and his gang of Satan's Wolves, Bobby changed gears and became quiet. Bobby knew this had to be one of the inmates Dan Burns wanted information on, as he had no other cellmate up until now after the meeting with Dan. Besides this jerk would usually be kept by himself, Bobby loved the challenge and knew he could take care of himself, if it got ugly.

Dirty Mike slept for an hour. When he heard the food trap to cell open and the deputy yell, "chows up" Dirty Mike made his way to the grab his tray. Bobby was careful to let Mike get the first tray passed into the cell to show respect. As they sat at the dayroom table, Bobby put his hands on his knees and pushed his tray away. Dirty Mike swallowed his rice and chicken and sneered at Bobby and said with food coming out of his mouth.

"What the fuck you don't like the food here? Give me that tray; if you ante goanna eat it. Bobby passed it over to Dirty Mike.

Bobby then started his act again "Just thinking, my bitch eating good out on the street and I'm eating this jail house shit. If it wasn't for her dumbass I wouldn't be here.

Dirty Mike burped and said I don't go to jail for no bitch. They go to jail for me. You got to keeps um in line, no horseshit."

Bobby looked concerned and said "I need to be like you, and then my women would know to stop her drama. Bet you keeps um all straight?"

Dirty Mike talked most of the night about how he never let a women ever talk shit to him. Then Bobby said "did you ever have to ice one?"

Dirty Mike never missed a beat he was on a roll and he felt comfortable. "I stabbed one for making my eggs wrong and I shot one for money. That's the way you got to do um.

Bobby kept a straight face and continued to get the hit man to talk. "You work for the top dogs player, that's heavy. But you probably keep low around Tampa?"

"Keep low, my ass, I did a bitch for a Russian dude, not long ago here. Highbrow bitch. One shot of a .45 to finish her ass. Dumped her under the overpass. Never forget, I work anywhere in this city. They want some a problem solved they come see Dirty Mike."

"You the man dude, you the man." Bobby laid back down on his bunk he had just heard the dumb fool confess to a murder for hire. Bobby had the information on the murder Dan needed.

Bobby waited for a deputy to make his patrol around the jail floor and waved him over to the cell.

"Hey deputy, my stomach is killing me can I need a nurse."

The deputy wanted no sick inmates on his watch so he told Bobby to get his uniform on and "come to the gate".

Once outside the cell and down the hall out of site, Bobby told the deputy, "I need to make a call to a detective about a murder"

The deputy gave Bobby an exasperated look and said "oh my god, this better be no bullshit, Lets go see the Sergeant."

After talking with the Jail Duty Sergeant in his office, Bobby was given a phone call. He dialed Dan's cell.

Dan was lifting weights on his back patio, a routine he practiced to keep his head and body sharp, his cell rang and he recognized the jail number. He answered immediately "Burns". He knew Bobby' voice when he heard "Lieutenant Burns its me."

Bobby felt a bit of pride with his work and said "I have your information, all you need. The creep confessed to me. All the details, this one, thinks he's the cat's meow and smarter than any cop."

Dan heard the strength in Bobby's voice and felt exuberant for him. He knew Bobby just might make it. "O.K. I'll call the State Attorney and get you placed on R.O.R. (release) and Bobby stay in touch, I'll need your testimony."

Bobby replied with the street savvy that he used when he was a working undercover narcotics cop, "Most definitely."

Dan called his girlfriend and Assistant State Attorney Lisa Jones. He was brief and kept conversation very professional. "Counselor I need a prisoner released and a deposition done immediately on an Inmate Bobby Dobbins. He will sign an affidavit that will clear a murder."

Lieutenant, Lisa said just as professionally, I'll call the Circuit Judge and get him released and transported to the your office for an interview. This one will be your responsibility so don't let anything happen to him."

"He will be under constant watch….. Oh and thanks for your help." Dan hesitated a second and added, "a cocktail at 7:30, Steak and eggplant at 8:00?"

"On the rocks and a big thick chewy New York Strip, see ya." Lisa said so unprofessional.

CHAPTER - 12

The new charge of murder had been placed on Dirty Mike and when he was advised he was taken by surprise. He figured "Smiley" Baker must have snitched on him, since Baker had been the driver of the van, he used when abducting the young Air force Lieutenant. Baker witnessed him when he shoot the girl, and dumped her body under the overpass. He remembered Baker had been caught in a drug raid and was in jail. Dirty Mike knew Baker might try to deal his way out of doing any time in the prison. Dirty Mike had given "Smiley" Baker orders to get rid of the gun he shot the girl with, but they both had gotten wasted on oxy and whiskey. Dirty Mike figured "Smiley" might have kept the gun to sell, dumb bastard he should have killed him. He wondered if the cops had the gun?

Dan and Lisa Jones waited in the jail lobby of the interview area until Dirty Mike was in the interview room at the jail for twenty minutes to get him pissed off and angry at waiting. He asked the deputy guarding the interview area to tell Dirty Mike a detective was waiting to see him but he had to finish his cigarette outside which was a lie because Dan didn't smoke but he knew he needed an edge with the biker psychologically. Dirty Mike boiled over the comment. He slammed his cuffed hands on the table. Dan watched him from the outside the interview room through the door window. He then went inside the room by himself and began his interview with Dirty Mike.

"Good morning sir, How are you? Let me just turn on my tape recorder. I'm Lieutenant Burns and you're being charged for the murder of Dawn Ross. Let's get this over with I'm in a hurry got a lunch date with my squeeze. Let me read you your rights."

Dirty Mike was boiling angry at having waited for this cop to smoke a cigarette a habit he loved and was denied because there was no smoking in jail, then leave him sitting, and hear about lunch with a bitch. Nobody, least of all a cop would get away with treating Dirty Mike like a piece of shit.

The biker's anger was too much to control, he couldn't stand anymore and began yelling "Fuck you man, I know my fuckin rights. I done time, I don't wait for no cop to smoke a cigarette on my time.

Dan knew his strategy worked on the psycho biker.

"So you waive your rights," asked Dan quietly rolling his eyes. When Dirty Mike saw Dan roll his eyes, he went crazy, he jumped up and yelled "yes I killed the bitch and I'll kill your ass, you fuckin pussy ass cop."

Dan had him, this was what he had hoped his taunting the biker would lead to, he pressed on.

"Yes you shot her and then you took her body and dumped her like a piece of garbage under the Dale Mabry overpass. But you killed her for somebody else, somebody who is outside enjoying the best of life while you rot in here."

Dirty Mike heard the words, "somebody else", "you rot in here". His brain went into the survival mode. He tried to control himself but was overcome with anger.

"Yeah I was doing a job, the bitch was set up, taken to the a night club, led outside like clockwork, pushed into a van and taken for a ride. Baker was driving, that bastard the one who dimed me out to you? He's got the gun she was smoked with."

Dan opened the door of the interview room, stepped outside into the hall and asked the deputy to tell the State Attorney waiting in the jail lobby to come to the interview room. S.A. Lisa Jones walked up to Dan and he looked at her and said "He admitted to killing the girl, had an accomplish, and says he was hired to do the murder."

Lisa entered the room with Dan and said "Mr. McGee I am State Attorney Lisa Jones, I am prepared to offer you a deal in exchange for your truthful testimony of the murder of Dawn Ross and who hired you to kill her.

Dirty Mike still boiling with anger heard the words of the Prosecutor and realized he needed to deal with her immediately.

Mike felt a bit of sweat on his chest as he started to regain his composer and said "It's the Russian, I did the job for. He's runs this city now, he told them Latin's who was in charge. I don't know his name, fancy dresser; top of the line car, always has plenty of muscle with him. I have your word you will protect me from them? These people don't blow smoke."

Lisa spoke with authority. Mr. McGee you will spend a long time in prison, you will be protected and eventually you will be back on the street. You're testimony and its results are in your best interest, so tell me all you can and don't lie to me or frabricate anything. The minute your story starts to smell, you're on your own, and I don't think you'll get along to well on your own."

Dirty Mike under oath told Lisa everything he knew, while a court reporter recorded everything he said. He explained how the Russians hired him, how Dawn Ross was set up and how Baker his fellow biker, drove the van and was given the gun to get rid of. Dan checked with the jails Central Booking who verified Baker was in jail. He called the evidence room at Tampa Police HQ and the pistol Dirty Mike described was listed on the property inventory sheet of the biker Baker who Dirty Mike said he gave the gun too. Baker was in jail, picked up cooking dope for the Russians in the Afgan heroin raid in the Gardens. The gun would be tested for ballistics and it would match the bullet found in Dawn Ross' head. Lisa had a solved case or so she thought. Dan made a phone call to the Chief Ortiz and Sergeant Ross answered.

"Ross this is Burns, tell the Chief ...we got are man"

Ross knew immediately the case Burns was referring, "that will please her; she has a briefing with the Mayor at 1500 hrs."

The Chiefs secretary Jane listened on her extension and also knew the case Lieutentant Burns was referring to. She called the man who was helping her daughter, knowing it was wrong but she needed the money for her daughter Boris always gave her for her information.

CHAPTER - 13

The phone rang and Boris punched the answer bar recognizing the number. It was Nick Harmon. Boris said nothing, he just listened

Harmon sounded concerned; He was always right to the point.

"The police have the biker; we need to make sure he keeps his mouth shut."

Boris was amused at the American Intelligence agent being worried about the operation. Typical American attitude, wants to be rich and powerful, but they were always worried about the way things looked. Doing business with these people was a laugh. Americans were phony.

They always acted like they were superior to others, but they had no heart when it came to consequences.

Boris spoke with a calm voice, "yes I was informed by a friend, don't worry the biker will be taken care, he will be a good fellow."

Nick became angry at his lack of concern, "You should have let us taken care of the girl. Having her murdered and dumped for the police to find her, was amateurish, this is not Moscow. Your actions have now created a problem that could have been avoided. Bringing attention to your organization before you completed your operation for Mr. Jones clients was stupid. You need to take care of this problem before it gets out of hand. Don't make any more blatant mistakes."

"My friend it will be fine", Boris hung up the phone and he calmed his anger by finishing his vodka on ice.

Boris looked at the three former Spetznaz men, Goddard Mikel, and Ivan turned mafia enforcers for the organization. They had been smuggled into MacDill Airbase on Captain Sherman's boat and driven by Sherman, to Boris's condominium. They stayed at the condominium and they carried out the beatings and murders of those in the Tampa underworld who balked at the Russian gang taking over their criminal operations.

They had just returned from the streets of Tampa were they had beaten several bar owners who had resisted Demetri's extortion of their gambling and prostitution operations. They sat comfortably on a sofa, in the luxurious condominium of Boris' checking their pistols and adjusting their holsters, drinking good Russian vodka. They raised their glasses to Boris who toasted them with his glass. Boris had another assignment for them. He went to his desk, thumbed through a drawer of counterfeit documents and handed Goddard an official Lawyers Bar card in the name of Jeffery Thomas.

Boris explained to his associate "Put on a plain suit from my closet and take an empty attaché case from the shelf. You and I are going to visit the county jail, where you will present this card to the officer at the reception desk."

Goddard studied the card for a moment and memorized the name.

"Tell them want to speak with a prisoner named Michael McGee, who you represent. Carry no weapons as you will have to pass through a metal detector. When they bring him to see you, they will place you in a private conference room with him. Take his life quietly with your hands. Ensure he is sitting back in his chair. Exit the room as if nothing has happened. Leave the way you came in. I will wait in the car with Ivan and Mikel. The place is busy and no one will detect anything until you leave, believe me. They never question a lawyer in the jails of America."

Goddard laughed, finished his vodka, looked at Boris with a wry smile "This man will not enjoy his legal advice from me."

Boris then spoke to Mikel and Ivan, "We have a bail bonds company securing the release from jail of another one of the bikers of the Dirty Wolves. You and Ivan will follow him when he is released from the jail and kill him. He likes the whiskey and women, so he will go straight to the bars, he and his comrades frequent. I will drive you there and park down the street. When he leaves the bar follow him out in the darkness and kill him. He will be stupid from the liquor and not able to struggle. Then we can get rid of his body with no trouble."

CHAPTER - 14

Dan contacted Interpol and they identified the Russian crime boss Demetri and his right hand man Boris, but was unable to identify the other men with them in the pictures Johnny had taken at the port. Interpol had tracked Demetri and Boris leaving Russia, immigrating to Western Europe, Israel and then America.

Dan called Dennis Brightwater the O.S.I who had been working with Hanson in the murder of Lieutenant Ross. Brightwater was in his office on the base and answered the phone on his desk.

"Dennis, Lieutenant Dan Burns Tampa P,D, Sergeant Mike Hanson works for me and am gonna e-mail you some pictures of some military personnel, I believe are from MacDill."

"Send em, Lieutenant, Hope I can be of service."

Brightwater identified the military members stationed on MacDill. Major Curtis Long Special Operations Green Beret. Army Colonel Jacob Martin Special Operations Green Beret and Air force Colonel Jeffrey Crenshaw MacDill Commander of fight operations.

Dan pondered the situation, what were a C.I.A officer, two Green Berets and the flight operations officer of MacDill A.F.B. doing in a ware house with members of the Russian mafia? This smelled bad and Nick Harmon being in town made things really raw. Was this a C.I.A. Military operation? The meeting at the port warehouse? The Russian thugs, drug traffickers, who were attempting a takeover of organized crime in Tampa in the last month. The murder of Air force Lieutenant Dawn Ross was contracted by the Russians, but why? The money and the schedules found in her safety deposit box, pointed to her working for the Russians, but why was she killed? The Bikers testimony would be enough to bring in the Russians on a conspiracy to murder, then a search warrant for the warehouse to be searched and see if the crates held any contraband. Dan needed to call Johnny Creasy to see if his surveillance on the Russians and Nick Harmon had turned up anymore interesting aspects.

CHAPTER - 15

Dirty Mike was found dead in an attorney client room at the jail. His neck was broken. He was sitting in his a chair, leaned up against the wall. An attorney had come to the jail produced a bar card, requested to see inmate Mike McGee and left. Deputies who were busy escorting inmates to and from the attorney visitation area found the dead biker after noting the inmate by himself in the room for a longer period of time. The front desk checked the computer sign in records of attorneys visiting clients for the day and found Dirty Mikes attorney to be a phony name.

Dan was contacted by Lisa who was with Sheriff's detectives at the murder scene.

"Lisa how the hell did they let him see a lawyer when he was in protective custody". asked Dan

"It was an oversight, guy shows up, tells him he's a lawyer, shows a bar card and the staff doesn't want to violate any rights. He gets the guy in the attorney visiting room and does him in. Looks like a karate chop to the neck. Our dirt bag witness never knew what hit him. Oh one more thing the deputy that checked our "lawyers" bar card and allowed him to see the inmate, said the guy had a funny accent."

"Would he know a Russian one if he heard it?, Any Prints found?"

"Yeah about every inmate and other lawyer who has used the room, it will take a long time to track them all down." Lisa said with aggravation in her voice.

"There's more bad news. I went to put a hold on the custody of Gus "Smiley" Baker and he was already bonded out by a bonding company. The company received payment and posted the bond. Baker gave the clubhouse address to the bonding company as his residence. Our investigators went to the club house to pick him up and nobody in the place knows where Baker is"

"Lisa these are pro hits, and the Russians did it. They were alerted McGee was rolling on them on the Ross killing and they slienced him. They knew Baker was the wheel man for McGee and they hit him after he was bonded out of jail. Our case is beginning to look like history. We've got a leak. Lisa this is a hot mess, I'll get back to you thanks and be careful."

Dan immediately called Ron Becker on his cell who was relieving Johnny Creasy on surveillance of the port warehouse.

"Ron. Burns here anything new on the port warehouse?"

Lieutenant as we speak I'm following an Air force tractor trailer with the crates aboard entering the gates of MacDill Air force Base. The truck is right behind a lead car with uniformed military officers who were directing the loading at the port."

"Ron the biker McGee was murdered at the jail and I'm sure the transfer of the crates after the meeting we monitored at the port has some kind of link to this whole messy affair. I don't quite know what yet."

Dennis Brightwater was at MacDill Security Police Office putting up a law enforcement flyer on the bulletin board requesting information anyone may know about the death of Lieutenant Ross. A young Security Police Airman,

Tim Johnson was getting a coke out of the machine in the Lobby and recognized the late Lieutenants picture on the flyer and remarked to Brightwater.

"That's a dam shame about Lieutenant Ross. O.S.I. got anything yet."

Brightwater looked at the base cop and shook his head, then said, "I only wish I could tell you yes, but this case is very cold."

Johnson patted his holstered pistol and said "she was beautiful. She rode through my gate a few times in the sweetest red Mustang with some Captain leaving the base a few times. Always late at night, figured they were headed out to enjoy the night life."

Brightwater had to steady himself as he was overcome with adrenalin. "What Mustang and what Captain. Do you know the Captains name.?"

Johnson could hear the excitement in the O.S.I. agent voice, "It's a cherry red Mustang, Not sure of his name. Like I said, saw them a few times together in his car passing through the main gate at night. The Captain must have a ton of money, has a killer boat tied up at the dock on the base beach. I've seen him coming in late at night with some others, from fishing trips. He's a pilot, I've seen him on the flight line do a systems check with a crew chief on a F-16."

Johnson you have a keen eye, don't tell anyone what you have told me, I'll be in touch with you later about identifying who was on the boat with him. Good job, now remember nothing about our conversation."

"Yes Sir." Johnson watched as the O.S.I. agent hurried out of the building and sped away in his car.

CHAPTER - 16

Dennis Brightwater called Mike Hanson and explained to him the information he had received. Hanson told to meet him a Bennies Café in an hour. When he arrived he was surprised to see a man and women sitting with Hanson.

Hanson waved Brightwater over to the booth and introduced him to the man and woman.

"Dennis this is Chief of Police Jennifer Ortiz and Lieutenant Dan Burns."

"Hello Chief it's a pleasure to meet you and Lieutenant we finally meet in person instead of talking on the phone."

Dan motioned to the waitress and asked her to bring a cup of coffee for Dennis and a refill for Mike and the Chief.

Dan began "Mike told me what you have learned, have you checked out the Captain who was seen with Lt. Ross?"

"Yes, I found a Captain Sherman through the base pass and I.D who was issued an officers sticker #123 for a cherry red Mustang. He's a jet jockey, been on the base for about six months. Enlisted in 2000, tours of duty in Iraq and Afganistan, number of times. His last assignment was Airbase Bravo Afghanistan, during the time Lieutenant Ross was there. Get this, Base Personnel records show they both requested MacDill after the yearlong tour in Afghanistan. They arrived weeks within each other. Sherman lives on base, in officers housing. Everybody I talked to at Ross's squadron said she was a loner, no boyfriend, but I got a base cop puts them together, leaving the base at night together.

The Chief looked at Dan, then at Dennis and said "can you pull Sherman in for an interview with us?"

Dan put his hand up and stopped Dennis from answering, "Chief I requested you to meet us here because I want everything in this case going forward to remain classified. I'm sure the Russians hit McGee and Baker.

Somebody leaked McGee was rolling over on them on the Ross murder. They also knew about Baker being a co-conspirator with McGee and he's bonded out of jail and disappeared. No doubt he's dead. The leak could have come from somebody at the sheriff's office, our department, or the State Attorney's office. Like I told you, I have reason to believe a C.I.A. Agent named Nick Harmon is involved in this affair. Harmon has access to a lot of information, due to his position and the Russians may have somebody on the inside their paying for information on our moves. Harmon was seen with the Russians and three Military officers in a warehouse on the Port of Tampa. They were very chummy, checking some large crates marked U.S. Government property. I checked on the invoice from one of the crates and nobody knows anything about them from there original destination the Aberdeen Proving Grounds. Last night the military transferred the same crates onto MacDill Air Base. Whatever is in those crates is the connection between the Russians, Nick Harmon, the C.I.A., and the Military. Sherman is our only lead to the Russians in the murder of Ross. I don't want to spook him. Once we pull him for an interview, if he's dirty, he could disappear, and our case goes cold again. We find out why the Russians murdered Dawn Ross and we may just open Pandora's Box. I want to set up surveillance on Sherman. Dennis covers him on base with our help and also tries to find out what's in the crates and where on base there being stored. Nobody but my unit, Dennis and you Chief, knows what we are doing. We keep everything under cover until we are ready to break this thing wide open. Nobody gets a clue, not with a possible leak."

Chief Ortiz looked at Dennis Brightwater and asked "can you get us on base without anybody knowing what's going on?"

"I can. I sign Mike on as Paul Perry a former college friend, here to visit me from South Dakota. I'll have an entry pass issued to him for a week's stay and a temporary sticker for the car he drives."

Dan added "Great cover and Denise Ramstein will come as Mike's wife. They can keep an eye on Sherman and tail him on and off base. Mike check out a confiscated car from the Police garage to use, and get Florida rental plates in the name of Paul Perry. Corporal Brady has authorization to register phony plates in the D.M.V. computer in case somebody enquires.

Mike Hanson laughed and said. "Now I'm a black guy from South Dakota,...... Denise's new squeeze."

The Chief looked at Brightwater and said "Dennis whatever is in those crates has been transferred to the base. It's a Federal government problem, but according to Dan, with C.I.A. Agent Harmon in the wood pile, the woods rotten. I would advise you to be careful how you handle the problem. We want the Russians for murder. Your butts out in the wind, if this thing goes south."

Brightwater scoffed "yeah but maybe you'll hire me if the Air force cans me.

CHAPTER - 17

Demetri sat in a dark booth with a glass of cold vodka enjoying the atmosphere of one of his newly acquired dance clubs. He listened to the hip hop music and watched a young beautiful women on stage swing her body on a cold dance pole. A cocktail waitress came over to the table and handed him a note given to her by a large man who resembled a professional fighter. After reading the note, he motioned to his two body guards to be alert. The note was from Mr. Jones directing Demetri to go to a limo parked outside the club, pronto. Demetri walked outside and entered a limo parked at the front door of the club. He entered into the comfortable leather seat of the limo and found himself looking into the eyes of the mysterious Mr. Jones, who was really a man named Herman Levovitch member of the "Stahl".

"Demetri, again I find you enjoying the better things in life. You have become so prosperous here in Tampa. You have done well the last few months ... in charge of this sunny city. My congratulations... and of course the money my clients have paid you has put you, shall we say, ahead of the competition."

Demetri felt himself sink deeper into the cushy leather seat. He felt the one thing in the presence of this man, even after so many years in the Russian Gulags, Demetri felt fear. He swallowed hard and said, "Yes of course, my operations have been successful and I am ready to complete your work, but I have heard nothing from you." My people are in place ready for your instructions to smuggle the suitcases."

"My people have been watching you and we are aware of the former commandos working for you. I assume they will make the delivery of the suitcases we have discussed?" Levovitch didn't wait for a response to his question "In three nights your men will meet with our contact from the C.I.A. Nick Harmon. He will transport your men to the Airbase. A Lear jet under C.I.A. authorization, with clearance from the Base Operations Flight Commander, will be allowed to land at the base. The nuclear suitcases are being stored in a hanger on the base. They are being guarded by C.I.A. contractors who work for us. Your people will board the plane along with two Army Green Beret, a Colonel and Major, who will fly with your men, to the U.S Air force Base Aviano in Italy. They will see your men and the suitcases are provided a truck for transportation and escorted off base. Once off the base, your men will be given cell phones with numbers for the local police, who work for us, to provide escort for you to your smuggling route. Once your men are in position there will be no further assistance from our organization. You will be responsible to see your men smuggle the suit cases to the capital cities of the countries we have discussed and detonate them when they receive a coded message on the cell phones from our operatives."

"It will be no problem, we will contact our people in Italy and they will make arrangements to meet and smuggle the men and suitcases to their destinations when they leave the base." Demetri smiled but knew the operation had to succeed or he would become hunted by these people.

Herman Levovitch stared hard at Demetri, with his madman expression. He enjoyed squeezing others. "See everything is as we discussed. Now go Demetri and please, I expect no excuses or problems."

Bill Barton sat in his car on surveillance in the parking lot, watching as Demetri exited the limousine and returned to the club. He pressed the transmit button on his portable radio, "Indigo 3 to Tango 1 suspect back into drinking establishment after meeting with unknown person."

Dan received the message and transmitted to Johnny, "Tango to Indigo 5 stay on Demetri. Indigo 3 pick up a tail on the suspects visitor and find out who's riding in the limo."

Johnny who was parked in his car, across the street from Demetri's club, spoke into his portable radio, "10-4, Lieutenant. I'm stuck on my friend Demetri."

Bill Barton followed the limo to a private Airport and watched as the passenger got out and departed into the awaiting Lear Jet. He radioed to Dan on the police radio in the car, "Indigo 3 to Tango, suspect boarded a private jet, the bird has flown the coop."

CHAPTER - 18

Denise Ramstein and Mike Hanson kept a rotating surveillance on Captain Sherman. He left his quarters at 0800 in the morning like clockwork, arriving at his flight instructors job at the base F-16 simulator, returning to his quarters at 16:15 hours. His only outside stops seemed to be the commissary where he bought a large amount of groceries and the package store buying a lot of liquor. Dennis Bridgewater had spoken to an Air force Security Police Sergeant working a base patrol and new the cop would know about unusual things happening on the base which could lead him to the where the crates were being stored.

"Sergeant Wiggins, How have you been?

"Hello Sir. Just maintaining, ready to get this shift over and spend some time with the wife."

Dennis started the conversation with praise for the Sergeant, "Time off is a wonderful thing, Hey I saw the report you authored on the Airmen you caught gassing up his POV with gas from the motor pool pumps. I can't believe the people in motor pool left the gas pump unlocked. Great job".

"The Sergeant laughed. He felt proud being recognized for his apprehension of the gas thief by the O.S.I. Agent. "Thank you Sir, First time I saw a ten year old pickup truck being passed off as an Air force vehicle."

After breaking the ice with the cop Dennis asked asked "Sergeant, you heard about any shipments brought onto the base under heavy security and maybe where they have been taken.

The Sergeant thought for a second, Oh yeah you mean Hanger 5. They have the place sealed up tight. I heard they brought a tractor trailer there and unloaded inside the Hanger. Special Forces officers ordered the place off limits to everybody. They have two guys with C.I.A. badges armed with MP5's and Glock side arms guarding the place. Word is Top Secret stuff. Court martial if you get caught snooping around Hanger 5. But hey you the O.S.I. man, you got the juice to find out."

"Sergeant, thank you for your time, Nice seeing you and have a good one." The shipment was in Hanger 5 and Dennis knew he had to find out what it was, its importance, and confiscate it.

Dennis called Dan Burns on his cell and when Dan answered he broke the news.

"Lieutenant, good news, found the crates, bad news guarded by armed C.I.A."

CHAPTER - 19

Two nights later, Detective Sergeant Mike Hanson relieved Office Denise Ramstein of her surveillance of Captain Sherman, who was presently in his quarters. An hour into the watch Sherman and another man left the base apartment and left in Sherman's red Mustang. Hanson followed them to a parking area in front of the Base Exchange where they parked and sat in the car. After fifteen minutes Hanson knew something was strange. He used his cell phone to call Dennis Brightwater and Denise, who were both at Brightwaters quarters.

Dennis answered. "Hello"

"Dennis" Mike sounded uneasy, "I have Sherman and another guy together in a car outside the base exchange, Looks like a possible meet with someone."

Dennis felt his adrenalin flow, "Denise and I are on our way."

Dan Burns was watching Nick Hanson leave the downtown Federal Building in a white van with government plates. He followed him staying several car lengths back. Johnny Creasy was in another car alternating the tail to ensure Nick didn't spot them. The van arrived at a high rise condominium on the west side of Tampa and entered the parking garage. The condominium was luxury all the way. Dan parked in the street and waited for a minute and then drove into the garage. He saw the parked van and Nick Harmon going into an elevator. He parked a few rows over from the van slumped down in the seat to stay out of sight. Several minutes later Nick, Boris and three men with dressed in jeans turtle necks and carrying heavy coats came out of the garage elevator. Demetri was with them and he and Boris shook hands and Demetri drove out of the garage in a sedan by himself. Boris, Nick, and the three Russian hit men entered the government van. Dan picked up his radio and transmitted

"Indigo 5 this is Tango. The van has five with the driver and pulling out, stay on them."

Johnny transmitted back "10-4, 10-56."

Johnny followed the van down the Dale Mabry Avenue without being detected. The traffic was heavy and Johnny stayed behind a few car lengths with a keen eye on the van. The van proceeded down Dale Mabry and approached the main gate of MacDill Air force Base. Johnny pulled over off the road into a bank parking lot outside of the gate and radioed Dan. "Indigo 5 the suspect has arrived and entered destination, MacDill"

Colonel Jacob Martin and Major Curtis Long arrived at Hanger-5. Martin and Long were wearing web belts with a holstered Beretta .45 and three extra clips. Martin was exuberant with the thought of the devastation of the terrorist enemy he had fought with all his being, the last ten bitter years. The military was his life, a career Green Beret officer, Martin was now in charge of a counter terrorist unit in the Special Operations Command at MacDill. The military life had been good, but was now too much of a contradiction to accept with the refusal of the politicians to let the military fight the war on terrorism the proper and only way, with brute force. Martin was tired of seeing young men and women coming home with loss of limbs and ending up in a mental health ward in the V.A. because the politicians who controlled the Pentagon sold them out and refused to defeat the enemy in the middle east. A decorated combat solider, Martin meet a high level American diplomat who was also feed up with the how the war was fought and recruited Martin and his best friend and deputy unit commander Major Curtis Long who was Martin' loyal disciple into the Stahl. Martin had real power, the kind the boys at the Pentagon would never give him, being a member of the Stahl. He received his orders from the organization, plus a Swiss bank account they filled up for his work. The C.I.A. Lear jet had landed and was being refueled to transport Martin, Long, the contraband, and Russians to the base in Italy. The clearance and the orders for the Lear jet and it scheduled landing and takeoff were arranged by high level members of the Stahl working in the C.I.A. and Colonel Jeffery Crenshaw the base flight operations officer who was also a member of Stahl. Crenshaw had received the orders, and arranged for the nuke suitcases to be stored in Hanger 5 under C.I.A. guard until the Lear jet landed and took off with its contraband load. Martin and Long ordered the C.I.A. guards to open the hanger doors. Air force loadmaster personnel where ordered by Crenshaw to load the suitcases onto the Lear jet that had taxied in front of the hanger after being refueled. Martin looked at his watch; the Russians should be here with in the next fifteen minutes.

CHAPTER - 20

Robert Sherman and the Russian Thomas Gold sat in the parking lot of the Base Exchange and waited to Ronda view with Nick Harmon and the Russians. Sherman was nervous and pressed Gold to tell him who they were waiting for.

"What is going on, who are we to meet here, is this even safe? Why don't I drive you off base to Boris?"

"Boris will be here soon and I will depart Captain. You will receive more direction from Boris after he arrives."

"I'm done, taking orders, after this I am disappearing, I plan to leave this country and live a long rich life in another part of the world. Captain Robert Sherman is going to retire early and never be heard from again."

Nick Harmon drove the van to the main gate of MacDill Air force Base and the gate guard saw the government plates on the van and looked at the C.I.A. credentials Nick flashed. The gate guard waved the vehicle onto the base. Harmon turned around smiled and looked at Boris and the three Russians, Goddard, Mikel, and Ivan, sitting in the back of the dark van. The van proceeded down the main drag of the base and pulled into the base exchange parking lot and alongside of Sherman' red Mustang.

Denise and Dennis arrived at the Base Exchange parking lot and exited Dennis' car. Moving fast they got into the backseat of Mike Hanson's car. Hanson handed Brightwater a pair of night vision binoculars and pointed to the Red Mustang on the other side of the lot.

Brightwater took a look and saw Sherman and his passenger. He handed the binoculars to Denise and she scanned her prey. Just as she started to put the binoculars down the van with Nick Harmon, Boris and the three Russians pulled up.

Denise recognized Harmon and Boris as they got out of the van.

"What have we got here, a meet of some kind, Sherman and Boris are shaking hands."

Brightwater pulled his Sig M-11 out of his holster and said "let's take um"

"Hold on cowboy, we got back up coming so let's wait. No sense in rushing this and getting shot."

Hanson picked up his portable police radio and transmitted, Sierra 1 to Tango we have suspects in parking lot of Base Exchange, red Mustang, white van, waiting on your arrival."

Dan entered the main gate in his car, flashed his badge and I.D. He told the S.P. gate guard he was on official police business and was working with O.S.I. Agent Dennis Brightwater. Johnny had parked his car on the side of the gate and jumped into Dan' car. Dan told the S.P. "Call your shift commander tell him Lt. Burns from T.P.D. needs back up at the Base Exchange and by order of the O.S.I. Hanger 5 is to be sealed off and the men their apprehended. Nothing moves from it make it pronto."

Dan and Johnny sped off and spotted the red Mustang and the white van.

Dan picked up his portable radio and transmitted to Mike Hanson, "Move in block them from leaving, Air force Police in route to back up."

Hanson answered "10-4."

Hanson drove the car up to the front of Sherman's car and Brightwater, Denise, and Hanson all moved out of the car with their weapons drawn and ordered Boris and Sherman to get on the ground and spread. The Russian Thomas Gold attempted to get out of the Mustang with his revolver drawn. Denise saw the metal of the gun and immediately turned her weapon on Gold. She yelled "Police" and ordered him to "drop the gun" but he turned toward her fast, raised the gun in her direction and fired. Denise felt the round go past her head and tapped her weapons trigger three times, hitting Gold with each shot in the chest. He fell to the pavement of the parking lot and lay dead in his blood. Nick Harmon tried to back the van up but Dan had pulled his car up directly behind the van blocking him. He ran to the window and placed his .45 pistol into the face of Nick Harmon.

"Place your hands out the window, now," Nick did as ordered. Dan opened the door and pulled Nick out onto the pavement. He saw the Russians in the back of the van and motioned to Johnny, "Put your hands behind your back." Dan placed his knee into the small of Nick's back and handcuffed him. Dan grabbed him by the collar of his shirt and pulled him away from the van, keeping his pistol aimed at the driver's side.

Johnny Creasy pulled open the passenger door and yelled to the three Russians but keeping his body out of their line of sight.

"Throw up your hands and move forward." A burst of automatic gun fire came from inside the van and blew the windshield out. Johnny jumped to the side of the van and landed on the ground firing his .45 into the vans panel seven times. Dan also fired his .45 into the van with six shots. Denise, Dennis and Mike fired into the van to neutralize the threat. The high impact rounds pierced the thin metal of the van and found the bodies of the three Russians knelling in the van trying to scramble out. A scream was heard from the van and then there was silence. Johnny screamed into the van again for the three Russians to come forward. Johnny approached the front of the van, keeping his weapon pointed into the van. He could see the shots had hit their Brightwater targets. The three Russian hit men lay in their blood. The overwhelming number of shots had been deadly. Air Force Military Police arrived and recognized Dennis wearing his O.S.I. badge on a chain around his neck. Brightwater directed them to place Nick Harmon in handcuffs.

Dan walked up to Robert Sherman and Boris, and pushed them both down on their knees and handcuffed them. Dan barked, "Boris Kozlov, you're under arrest for the murder of Lieutenant Dawn Ross. He read Boris his rights, then Sherman, and asked, "Do you understand these rights."

Boris looked at Dan with defiance, and refused to speak. Sherman nodded his head in the affirmative. Dennis Brightwater read Robert Sherman his Article 34 rights from the Military Code of Justice.

Dan looked over at Denise Ramstein and Mike Hanson and gave them thumbs up.

Dan placed a hand on the shoulder of Dennis Bridgewater and said. "You better get to the hanger and find out what these bastards were up to."

Dennis shook his head, "yeah, you are coming?"

"No, I'll take Boris, Sherman, and Harmon downtown to Police Headquarters I am charging Boris with the murder of Dawn Ross. He looked at Harmon and said

"I'm charging Harmon with being a piece of shit. He'll claim he's on an agency job and I'll get a visit from the F.B.I. and I'm sure they will have orders to take him to Washington. Maybe your people can raise hell with the C.I.A. and ask them why he has brought Russian hit men on your Airbase?"

Harmon was stunned and began to argue with Dan.

"Burns who the hell you think you are I'm a federal officer of the C.I.A and you're going to swing for your actions here. Now un cuff me at once you S.O.B."

Dan looked at Harmon, read him his rights and said "Nick you really do need a good lawyer."

"It's going to be one hell of a story," Dennis said as he motioned to one of the Air force Police officers who had arrived to scene, to give him a portable radio. He transmitted into the radio, "Agent Brightwater O.S.I. to Base Police, Surround Hanger -5 with all available units and don't let anything move from the area. I'm in route with a Base Police Patrol. Dennis looked at the two patrol officers and said "let's go, code four, Hanger -5" The car sped off, overhead lights cutting into the night and the sound of the siren wailing.

Dan radioed Jack Bradley and Ron Becker. "Get a Swat team and arrest Demetri. Bring him to Police Headquarters ASAP."

When O.S.I. Agent Dennis Brightwater and the patrols arrived Hanger 5 was surrounded by squads of Air Force Security Police. The crew and the plane Colonel Martin and Major Curtis were trying to board was seized. Colonel Martin realized they could not get away so he ordered the C.I.A. guards to stand down. When Dennis Brightwater and the Base Security Shift Commander checked the crates and saw the nuclear suitcases they placed Martin and Curtis under arrest. The F.B.I. was notified and took the men into custody and took over the investigation.

CHAPTER - 21

Boris and Harmon had been placed in temporary holding cells in Tampa Police Headquarters. Dan called Lisa and she arrived at the Police station. She authorized a deal for Captain Sherman, her Boss State Attorney Bernie Schwartz, had worked out with the on call Staff Judge Advocate who he immediately called, after Lisa informed him of the night's events. The deal, was immunity from the State Attorney's office for Sherman testimony against Boris, for the murder of Dawn Ross and his activity with Demetri's Russian criminal gang. He would be turned over the military authorities for Court Martial. Sherman waived his rights to an attorney, knowing his plight was futile, and accepted the deal for the testimony he was about to give.

Dan sat down at the table across with from Sherman and turned on the tape recorder. Sherman purged his soul speaking directly into the recorder testifying how he worked for the Russians criminal organization in Afghanistan and in Tampa. He admitted he and Dawn Ross left the base together to meet Boris at a nightclub in Tampa, where she disappeared after demanding more money from the Russians. Sherman was so matter of fact when he looked directly at Dan and Lisa and said "I knew when she left the table I would never she her again. The Russians were going to lead her to her death and I just sat there frozen, lost, and concerned not really too much for her but for my life and how much I wanted to leave alive."

He testified how he was paid money beyond his dreams to smuggle the Russian who called himself Thomas Gold, and the three others onto the base by boat. He admitted to driving Gold to the coffee shop, where Gold killed the rivals of the Russian organization at the order of Demetri. He admitted he transported the three other Russian gangsters off the base and delivered them to Boris, who employed them as enforcers and hit men.

Dan looked at Sherman and tried to understand how an educated man, a fighter pilot, a military officer, could sell his soul, his respectability, for money and watch as someone he had knew as a friend walked to her murder and he did nothing to stop it. So much mayhem was committed by criminals and Sherman was a major player in there takeover of city crime. Dan felt an instant dislike for Sherman and asked him a pointed question as he switched off the recorder, "Captain Sherman, do you think hell will even want you when your time comes?" Sherman looked at Dan the question penetrated his psyche. He sat in the interview room and wept long and hard. He was a broken man.

Dan met with his squad members the next morning and told them

"With your hard work we were able to close the Ross case. The Chief meet with the Mayor and reported the circumstances of the case. The Air force has denied knowing anything about the crates on their base taken from the port and the involvement of any other military personnel working with Demetri or his gang. They will investigate the information Sherman gave them but I have a feeling the whole story will never come out. Organized crime in Tampa for now is very much unorganized. The breakup of the Russians and the chaos they created with the other gangs in the city makes the situation a power vacuum and somebody will try and fill the top job. Give it a month and will have a front runner back in the game, flexing his muscle. So let's fill up the coffee pot and get started on the day's new events. Oh and by the way, make sure your reports are accurate. Be safe and watch your back."

EPILOGUE

Nick Harmon refused to make any statement after being arrested. He made a phone call and was released into the custody of the F.B.I. over the objections of the Tampa Police who's protest were met with a Federal Judge's order for his release. Harmon was immediately ordered to return to Langley Virginia C.I.A. headquarters. Several days later, his body was found floating in the Potomac River. He had been murdered by agents of the "Stahl" who made sure he would never tell who he was working for. Authorities called his death an accidental drowning.

Tampa Police Swat Team raided Demetri's house in Tampa but he was nowhere to be found in Tampa. A week later he was found dead in the trunk of a car in the Miami International Airport. He also was murdered by the "Stahl" Authorities in Miami had no suspects in his death. The Russian known as Goddard was identified in the morgue, as the phony lawyer who murdered Dirty Mike McGee in the jail. Robert Sherman was found guilty of espionage by the Air Force Court Martial and sent to a military prison for fifteen years under another name. Colonel Martin and Major Curtis were arrested and after weeks in the custody of the F.B.I. were forced to retire. They both left the country. The Pentagon worked to keep the whole affair as quiet as possible. Sherman's testimony for the State of Florida, against Boris at his trial was never needed. Boris was found hanging in his jail cell hours after he was booked into the County Jail. He was listed as a suicide. Boris had refused to make any statements about of the murder of Dawn Ross and the two Tampa crime lords who had been poisoned in the coffee shop and died. Boris along with the three Russian hit men, were buried as John Doe's in a grave yard in Tampa. The true identities of the men could never be confirmed and the Russian government refused to supply any information when requested by the United States Government. The murder of Gus "Smiley" Baker was attributed to the Russians by S.I.U. but there was never enough evidence to close the case.

Air force authorities confirmed phony orders were received from the C.I.A. for a plane to land at MacDill, refuel and proceed to a secret destination with its cargo.

The C.I.A. could never account for, who the orders came from. The Air force denied knowing anything about the type of cargo arriving on the base or being stored in Hanger 5. The C.I.A. refused any comment and said they were investigating the incident internally. Dennis Brightwater received a commendation for his actions for stopping what the Air force said were unauthorized civilians on the base and confiscating an illegal shipment. He separated from the Air force and joined the Secret Service.

The plot to bomb the cities Tehran Iran, Karachi Pakistan, and Khartoum Sudan was stopped on the Florida Air Base. The members of the "Stahl" were prevented from their plans to control the world for the time being.

Dan and Lisa spent a week relaxing, swimming and enjoying their time together at his condo on Clearwater Beach. After a week of vacation they returned to Tampa and their demanding work. Both of them knew the recent chaotic events, could have been a disaster for the world had it not been their solving the case of the dead Lieutenant. Tampa was a beautiful city, with a lot of crime, and they both knew there would be busy days ahead.

The End

39418239R00088

Made in the USA
Lexington, KY
22 February 2015